BLACKLIGHT CHRONICLES

BOOK THREE

SHADOW MAGE

JOHN FORRESTER

AMBER MUSE

ISBN-10: 0984825959

ISBN-13: 978-0984825950

Cover Design by Anca Gabriela Marginean

Visit: www.blacklightchronicles.com

1

The Rift

As the world spun wildly, Talis grasped at anything to stop his fall, but his fingers only sliced through the shimmering fog. He found himself sprawled on the ground, a hazy light bathing bright spring buds in the branches above. Someone was holding him down, and he glanced around groggily, realizing Mara was shaking him and slapping his face. He blinked. She yelled at him, her face frantic and desperate, but he couldn't hear a word she said.

His vision blackened and he found himself sinking backwards. He reached out, trying to steady himself, to hold Mara, hold something, anything to keep from falling again, but there was nothing to hold onto. He felt himself plummeting—arms and legs flailing—from darkness to quickly growing light, farther and farther, reaching jagged, menacing clouds.

"Mara!" he shouted, but his voice sounded deep and slurred and the wind whistled around him as he fell towards the ground.

He twisted and stretched, and the next moment he was standing on a vast plain dotted with boulders and stands of towering, alien trees. Talis squinted and stared. The trunks were banded with red razor-sharp limbs jutting out, holding limp emerald-colored leaves.

A whirlwind tumbled towards him, interrupting his fascination with the strange trees. The devil storm gathered strength and momentum, and Talis swore he glimpsed tortured faces within. He cringed and raised his hands to stop the assault, and the whirlwind froze just inches away.

Inside the churning storm Talis recognized one of the faces: Rikar. His old friend. A traitor to his own people. What had happened to him? Talis felt a chill staring at Rikar's pleading eyes. With a sudden *pop*, Talis's ears opened and he heard screams and moans and cries for help. A chorus of suffering. But one voice punched through the rest. Rikar's voice, low and clear. *Talis, you must help me. I'm sorry for everything I've done. I made a terrible mistake going with Aurellia.* Then Talis heard a tremendous hissing sound like thousands of vipers slithering in the dark. He clenched his hands over his ears, trying to make the sound stop.

Then Rikar's voice clear again. *Come find me…I'll die…worse than dying. Nikulo stole the scroll. Only you—*

Everything flipped inside out, spinning, and Talis was suddenly back in the swamplands again. Mara's hands covered her face, tears spilling through her fingers. Charna, Talis's pet lynx, nuzzled his hand and gazed at him with those mystical, golden eyes. *She really is a gift from the Goddess Nacrea,* Talis thought.

"What's wrong, why won't you come back?" Mara mumbled, her voice choked with tears.

"Mara…" His voice sounded like an old man on a deathbed. Talis coughed and cleared his throat.

She sprang forward and peered into his eyes. "Are you—"

"You didn't have to slap me so many times."

"I thought you were dead. You looked so pale after you touched the Surineda Map."

Talis stared at her blankly, trying to remember what had happened. The map, the vision, the other world.

Mara's eyes widened, and she hugged him. "Don't drift off again! My goodness, you're shivering. Stay with me." She lifted her eyes and glanced above at the wind stirring the branches and leaves. "Let's go home."

As they gathered their gear and prepared to leave, Talis grabbed Mara's wrist.

"I heard him." He sighed, remembering Rikar's tortured eyes.

"Who?"

"I had a vision of Rikar…he's out there…suffering. On that world we saw in the Surineda Map."

The City of Naru still looked bruised from the battle with the Jiserians. Their flying sorcerers had attacked several times in the last few months, but nothing like the massive battle months before. With the Temple of the Order of the Dawn destroyed, and the crystal underneath

6

broken, the wizards of the Order had little power to sustain fights against the invaders. Talis had learned to summon the power of the black crystal that lay beneath the Temple of the Sun, and only he and Master Jai fought together to defend their city. The other wizards refused to come anywhere near the temple.

As Talis and Mara sauntered through Naru's western gates, the soldiers backed away like they were infected by the plague. *A hero's welcome*, Talis thought. Worse every day. *They still hate the new temple, and mistrust the black crystal...* Now the opposition that the Order had expressed against Talis and the black crystal affected the royal House of Lei. Mara's family.

"We should probably split up now." Talis stared up at the city's massive stone arena.

Mara nodded, her face sad but resigned to hiding their friendship. "I'll see you soon?"

"Tomorrow...dusk...the temple?"

Her eyes glittered and she smiled, then turned and ran off towards Fiskar's Market.

Father looked bleary-eyed as Talis sat on the chair next to him and warmed his hands by the fire. He stared at the flames dancing around hickory wood. But in the silence Talis could feel his father's mind working.

"So the wizards of the Order tell me you're to blame for all the Jiserian attacks." Father scoffed in disgust. "And

7

House Lei dares to insinuate the Jiserian sorcerers are out to steal the black crystal?"

Talis bristled at the news. "They're going too far."

"I know, I know...but the people are listening. And Lady Malvia is furious that Mara is still spending time with you. Be careful, son, House Lei is not to be trifled with. Word is many of the Order are allied with them as well."

"Master Viridian too?"

Father shrugged and took a puff from his ornately-carved pipe. "Perhaps not. But the others may...."

"The black crystal saved our city." Talis said the words louder than he intended, and his father raised an eyebrow in response.

"No one but you and your friends seem to understand...only you experienced the Goddess Nacrea."

"And they disbelieve me still?"

"They hate what they don't understand." Father inspected Talis for a moment. "You look quite tired...unusual for you. What happened today out on the hunt?"

Talis shook his head. "Nothing," he lied. "I must have caught a chill."

"Then off to bed with you. Rest up, you have your studies tomorrow."

Although officially Talis was a student of the Order of the Dawn, since his journey the masters of the Order had issued him strange special assignments and forced him to study under old masters of forgotten magical arts. Not that he minded. He could stay away from his former classmates who now treated him as if he was an outcast.

After sneaking into the Order of the Dawn early morning through the side gate that led into the masters' chambers, Talis clambered down the steps to the dungeon that was Master Grimelore's workshop. As far as the other wizards were concerned, Master Grimelore spent too much time gazing at the fires that ever-burned in various stoves and heaths scattered throughout his voluminous workshop. He rarely left, insisting that the chill of the outside air might sap the Fire Magic from his body.

Master Grimelore emanated dry heat from his skin and hair and eyes. His face looked like a leathered lizard, with a nose that seemed better suited as a bird's beak. Instead of giving formal lessons, this morning Master Grimelore poked searing-hot coals with an iron stoker, his expression seemingly unsatisfied with what he saw. Obsessed with Fire Magic, but not fireballs or the summoning of flames, rather he focused on the art of channeling heat directly inside his enemies. Talis could attest it came in handy for keeping himself warm when he was out in the cold. Other wizards avoided Master Grimelore's eccentricities, claiming his kind of Fire Magic was messy.

"You should try some cardamon tea." The master waved his hand towards a ceramic pot on a small iron table. "Are we to spend our hour together studying or shall we play with the fire?"

Talis could tell from the wry glint in Master Grimelore's eye that they'd be learning how to draw heat from the roaring fire at the brick hearth. That part was easy. Holding it inside and containing the heat was an entirely different matter.

"Begin." Master Grimelore stoked the coals until they seethed with heat, and glanced at Talis out of the corner of his eye.

As Talis allowed the intense heat from the fire flow into his body, he built an invisible container to envelop the power. But pictures of flames melting his body to ashes caused his concentration to break. In a rush, he pushed the heat back into the fire and Master Grimelore jumped away from the hearth in surprise.

"What are you doing, trying to kill an old man? I know I've one leg stuck in the earth, minions of the Underworld feeding on my old bones, but do you really need to speed things up? I haven't even had my tea yet...."

"My apologies, master. I failed to contain the heat."

"I saw what happened." Master Grimelore wagged a finger, a mischievous look in his eyes. "You were thinking of that beauty of a girl...what's her name again? Mara? A young boy like you, of course you can't concentrate." He made an obscene gesture that made Talis believe his master was getting crazier by the day.

"Mara is a good friend."

Master Grimelore raised his eyebrows and stuck out his tongue. "Hah! A good friend, indeed. All those long days out on your adventure together, and you never once had any particular…urgings? It isn't so strange now is it?"

Talis felt his face flush, and he turned away to stare at the fire. Why would his master be thinking that? Did it show on his face when he thought of Mara?

"Ah now, my apologies for embarrassing you. That will be enough for today. When your mind is clear of all these *thoughts* we'll continue our lesson. For now, drink your tea and practice flame gazing."

As Talis sipped the delicious milky tea, he grabbed his thoughts and tossed them to burn in the fire.

"Breath in slowly until you feel a heaviness settle on your face…that's right, now let the air hiss out of your teeth. The fire cycling through your body—your lungs great baffles fanning the fire. Don't drift off now, don't get lost in drowsiness. Let yourself remain vigilant in the shadows under the flames."

Shadows under the flames, Talis thought. In his gazing, an inky-black mass bubbled out, covering his face and ears in a wet, sticky sensation. He dared not break his meditations, but felt revolted at the feeling. *Shadows*. Aurellia's face flashed in his mind's eye, laughing and mocking and hideous. *Shadows*. Rikar's tortured face trapped in the whirlwind.

Talis gasped, and opened his eyes in a panic. Master Grimelore stood towering over him. Talis somehow was lying on his back. The vision was true. Rikar was out there on that planet being tortured. An immense pressure fell over Talis's chest until he felt suffocated, with a knowing that he had to help Rikar. But considering all the terrible things Rikar had done, and his choice to follow Aurellia, the dark lord who devastated the Temple of the Goddess Nacrea, Talis knew that helping Rikar was a bad idea.

But if he didn't respond, if he ignored the call of Rikar and Aurellia, the shadows might rise up and overtake him, like the waves that washed over Onair and destroyed the city.

2

Rune Magic

In the eerie grey and silver light, the dank subterranean room smelled of clay and ink and fish oil. Barrels of the nasty tasting oil were stacked randomly in the corner of the chamber. Talis arrived late again for his least favorite subject: Rune Magic with Mistress Cavares, one of the oldest and weirdest of the wizards of the Order. And his afternoon studies included two hours trapped here in this dungeon.

"Have you memorized Galarian yet?" Mistress Cavares didn't even bother to look away from the tablet she was inscribing. She worked painfully slow inscribing the rune, as if one mistake could blow the whole room up.

Talis sighed. "My apologies, my lesson with Master Grimelore...ran longer than usual."

She finished and started chewing on a roasted snake. Talis's skin prickled at the crunching sound. She wiped her lips, but several shiny, green scales still stuck to the corners of her mouth.

"You must memorize both the language and the combinations." Her long, claw-like fingernails were painted purple with green swirls. She inscribed four characters on the rune, and each glowed after she lifted her hands from the small oval-shaped clay tablet.

Mistress Cavares had forced Talis to learn many ancient and discarded languages, mold clay tablets, and cast spells over the rune inscription. The rune combinations and bindings and unravellings baffled Talis.

"You see here, I'm doing a double rune, in Galarian." She studied his eyes. "What spell have I written and what is its level of power?"

"A double rune is the most powerful." Talis paused a minute as he struggled to decipher the characters. "Falling and...slow? Slow fall?"

She didn't even smile, although Talis knew he'd gotten it right. If he'd been wrong, she would have launched into another of her tirades about how incompetent he was.

"Mistress Cavares? Why do none of the other masters practice Rune Magic?"

She scoffed. "They're impatient—like you—and lack the diligence to learn the combinations and memorize the languages. They feel runes are too indirect compared to elemental magic. What they fail to understand is the subtlety runes offer to the skilled wizard."

"Like?"

"Have you ever heard of a magical ward?"

Talis shook his head.

"What in the world are they teaching students at the Order?" She sighed bitterly, and scraped a snake scale lodged between two yellowed teeth. "Do you want to remain ignorant your entire life?"

"I want to learn." Talis felt his skin crawl in anger, but he kept calm.

"Do you really now?" Mistress Cavares narrowed her eyes, studying him. "You've learned so little… You're heart's just not in it. Why should I teach you a thing?"

Talis realized his heart hadn't been in his studies. All this time he'd been spending with Mistress Cavares he'd been thinking of other things: his adventure, the Jiserians, the temple, and of course, Aurellia and Rikar. But had he really learned nothing? He looked down at the runes he'd inscribed the other day. Nothing perfect, but the knowledge of runes was slowly seeping in.

"But I have learned a lot." Talis softened his voice as he stared into Mistress Cavares's hard eyes. "Then again, perhaps my mind has been elsewhere. Ever since I've returned…it's like a storm cloud lingering over me. I never know when the lightning will strike."

"The war is over, child. At least that is what our astrologers tell us… Whatever power you summoned struck a vast blow against the Jiserian forces."

"But their sorcerers still attack us. And the Order scorns me. House Lei despises my existence. They think I lured Mara away from them."

Mistress Cavares shook her head and muttered to herself. "The Order… They hold much contempt for people that don't fit their mold of what a wizard should be, myself included. No matter, now. Let us not think of such things. Are you truly sincere about learning?"

Talis held her gaze. "I am serious about learning. But…can I ever do more than just learn languages and inscribe characters? What's this all for?"

"I have many secrets to teach. You could be the first apprentice who made it past this point. To possess the benefit of the ancient art of Rune Magic would grant you much power." She waved her hand at the runes scattered across the table. "These are merely instruments used in combination with an even deeper magic. Do you have what it takes?"

He felt suddenly determined to conquer the art of runes, despite what the others in the Order had said. But he could tell by the skepticism in Mistress Cavares's eyes that he'd have to prove himself.

"I will do more than try. I swear it upon the Goddess Nacrea—"

"Words, words… You're all the same with your words and empty promises. I want proof." She placed a three-character rune on the table. "Level of power and spell? Prove to me this knowledge you claim to possess."

Talis felt a trickle of sweat drip along his neck. The spell was inscribed in the words of the ancients, the most complicated language from the descendants of the destroyed City of Urgar. "Three-character rune…middling power. But written in the ancient tongue makes it similar to the two-character rune drawn in Galarian."

Mistress Cavares nodded her head. "Go on."

Talis frowned, not knowing the first character. "This character"—Talis pointed at the middle one—"is the sun in full power." The ancient language had three characters for the sun: rising, full, and falling. "The last character is…melting…or burning up?"

"And the first character?" Her face held the expression of someone who's caught a thief.

"I won't guess." He scratched the back of his head. "I don't know it."

Mistress Cavares puckered up her lips. "That's because I've never taught it to you. It means contained or more accurately…focused. To focus the power of the sun and melt something. Nasty little rune."

How is it nasty if it just sits there and does nothing? Talis thought.

"Now this rune you may have seen before." She fingered a four-character rune.

"A weak rune but very specific in nature. It means trap the intruder with a web of shadows. What exactly does that mean?"

Crinkles formed around Mistress Cavares's eyes. "Wouldn't you like to know…" She waved the idea away. "Show me your abilities in casting. I've seen you work against those Jiserian sorcerers, so I know you have some skill as a wizard. But can you contain it in focused amounts?"

"What spell should I cast?"

17

"Do you know how to cast a binding spell?"

Talis shook his head.

"Bind one form to another. Bind an intention or thought to an object. You do know what that means?"

"In theory. But I've never practiced it."

Mistress Cavares exhaled a hissing breath. "You blustering wizards, elemental magic…boom! All noise and hard power, but little internal strength. You're all just surface deep."

"Teach me. I want to learn the spell."

"I'll show you once. If you don't get it, I won't teach it to you again."

"But that's unfair!" Talis couldn't believe she was being so unreasonable.

"Life is unfair. The universe is a hard, cruel place. Deal with it." She raised a hand, aiming at a stone that lay on the table. "I will bind ice to this stone. It won't be permanent, but it will last for a long time."

She closed her eyes. "In my mind I see chunks of ice floating down a mountain stream. Thick piles of snow lay at either side. I feel the cold. It sinks into my bones. I can taste the chill as it rolls around on my tongue. With this complete sensation, I focus letting it flow from my mind, out my hands, and into the stone. Go!"

The stone spun around in circles. When it settled, frost slithered across the surface. Talis reached out and cautiously touched it. The stone was so cold Talis snapped his hand back in surprise.

"Now do it. Since you've master Fire Magic, imbue the same stone with heat. Your mind, your imagination. Bind to the stone."

Talis concentrated on similar specific images: a blazing forest fire, the smell of roasted spiders, smoke in his eyes from huts burning, heat surging in his chest. He opened his eyes and released it all into the stone. The table sizzled and spat swirls of smoke from the heat of the stone. Mistress Cavares glared at Talis as if he were mad.

"Where do you draw that kind of power from? The black crystal?"

"It's too far away." Talis gestured towards the fire in the hearth. "Master Grimelore taught me to bring in power from flames. And what I saw in my mind was what I've experienced before."

"Like the ancient tongue, close to the original source of truth."

What did she mean by that? She was always talking in riddles.

"You've succeeded in casting your first binding spell. It will be easier now for you to progress. But be warned, binding is all about your thoughts and imagination...so control yourself. A lazy, untempered mind makes a dangerous combination with bindings."

"What does this have to do with Rune Magic?"

"It's time for your first lesson." She motioned at the table. "The ancient art of casting magical wards." As she lifted a rune, slivers of silver light spidered out of her fingers and into the rune. "A magical ward is created through the combination of a rune and a binding spell cast upon the object on which that rune is drawn."

The light from her fingers grew stronger and bored into the characters etched on the rune. The clay tablet melted away into ash, and a faint glow of silver remained on the table. "The ward is locked onto the location where the rune lay. I've cast a Rune of Paralysis. The next person to touch this spot will be paralyzed. Care to try it?"

Talis shook his head and found himself stepping away from the table. He heard a meowing sound and glanced over just as Kalix, Mistress Cavares's cat, sauntered across the table.

"No Kalix!" Mistress Cavares said, and scooped up the cat. "You know you're not supposed to sneak inside my workshop." She scratch the cat's head and under his chin, and Kalix purred loudly.

Talis smiled and went to pet the cat, but his movement seemed to spook Kalix. In a sudden jerk, the cat leapt from Mistress Cavares's arms, and landed directly on the spot where the rune was placed. Kalix froze like a stuffed animal, eyes frightened, tail pointing straight up, body as rigid as a stone sculpture.

"My poor kitty," cried Mistress Cavares. She scrambled around Talis and held Kalix in her arms. "You must be more careful with Kalix, she spooks easily."

"Is she dead?"

Mistress Cavares sighed like she'd had enough of teaching him. "Don't you know what a Paralysis Spell does? It's temporary. Kitty will be fine in an hour or so. This isn't the first time he's stepped on a ward. He has a nose for finding them. One day I fear he'll step on the wrong ward...."

She stared into the fire, then sighed and lifted herself up. "Now it's your turn, prove your ability to cast wards. Choose the runes, practice on the table. And please try and keep your power down to a minimum. I don't want you blowing up the workshop."

3

Tandria Scroll

That afternoon Talis meandered towards the Temple of the Sun, thinking of magical wards. Could he set wards around the city to protect Naru? Did wards activate for anyone, or could you set them to go off only on enemies? Questions spun around in his head. He couldn't believe he was actually looking forward to his next lesson with Mistress Cavares.

The Temple of the Sun looked aged and weathered perched atop the newly created hillside, formed at the planting of the black crystal. Although it was only six months old, the temple complex seemed as if it had been there for hundreds of years. Flowers and grass blossomed all around, particularly around the black oak tree. The spring still nurtured the meadows and gardens around the temple.

Talis took a drink of the water and relished the sweet taste. As he stared up at the wooden temple, scenes of the old temple complex and the Goddess Nacrea played in his head. How he missed the Goddess. Her power and beauty and light. Would he ever see her again?

The City of Naru stood as a shadow lingering in the background, but sunbeams shone on the temple. Even when it stormed outside, sun always seemed to strike the temple, bathing it in radiant light.

Talis turned and spied Nikulo climbing the hillside. They clasped arms. "She's a beautiful temple," Nikulo said.

"I haven't seen you in ages…thought you'd abandoned me like the rest."

Nikulo chuckled. "Maybe I should've. You dragged us to the ends of the earth. And poor Rikar. Where is he now?"

The vision flashed in Talis's mind for a second. He sat, seeing Rikar's sad eyes staring at him.

"You alright?"

"Sorry, I was remembering a vision I had yesterday in the swamplands. I heard Rikar calling out to me, calling for help. He was trapped inside a storm filled with tortured faces. What's a vision like that supposed to mean?"

Nikulo shrugged and sat next to him. "How did the vision start?"

"The Surineda Map glowed and I touched it—Mara saw it too—the map showed us another world far away in the stars. I think he's out there, on that world." Talis glanced at Nikulo. "Rikar's in trouble."

Nikulo waved the idea away. "Trouble, indeed. He made the wrong choice the moment he decided to follow that sorcerer. But enough talk of our *old friend*. There was a reason I came to visit you. Do you remember the scroll I stole from Aurellia?"

Talis felt suddenly dizzy. *The scroll,* Rikar had said. "What about it?"

"I studied the Tandria Scroll for months after we returned. Hours and hours of translations. I finally discovered a poison spell written within and mastered it after weeks of study. But I ignored the other parts unrelated to Poison Magic. I left the scroll alone for awhile, but a few weeks ago, I found something."

"This is just too bizarre...."

"What?"

"Rikar told me in the vision that the scroll you stole from Aurellia was important."

Nikulo's face paled.

"What is it?" Talis said.

"Aurellia must have told him about the scroll. Why would he do that?"

"He's a master of deception. Perhaps he wanted you to find it. Think about it, he was leaving anyways." Talis thought a moment, then stared at Nikulo. "How did you find the scroll out of all the ones in his library?"

Nikulo looked nervous, as if he was caught in a lie. "I...I had visions of Aurellia before we reached Darkov."

"When? But you never told us a thing!" Talis couldn't believe Nikulo had kept it from him.

"He kept telling me about all he could teach me, about mind control and poisons...all the things I'm interested in."

Nikulo sighed and stared out over the Nalgoran Desert. "If we figure out how to decipher the characters on the scroll, we'll gain a rare spell. The true discovery inside the Tandria Scroll…is the knowledge of casting portal spells."

"Are you serious? A portal spell? So we could travel anywhere we wanted?"

Nikulo grinned. "Can you imagine?" He unfurled the Tandria Scroll, and tapped a finger on a part littered with archaic illustrations. "See…here are the portals. Going through walls, across rivers, to tall peaks. This looks like a summoning portal…calling someone to you."

"And what about this?" Talis pointed at an illustration of two figures aiming at a portal.

"This seems like the lead sorcerer…maybe bringing someone *along* with you through the portal? I don't understand all this."

Nikulo eyed cakes Talis's mother had packed for him in the morning before he'd left for the temple. "Are those apple tarts?"

"Pay attention! I thought you've been studying the scroll for months?"

Nikulo grunted at the cakes. "Just one?"

Talis rolled his eyes. Nikulo's stomach was always more active than his brain. "So what don't you understand about the scroll?"

"The language constantly changes…characters I don't know." Nikulo crammed the cake into his mouth. "I wink I unwerstand awout walf of it."

"Can you not talk with your mouth stuffed with cakes?" Talis shuddered at the pieces dribbling from Nikulo's mouth. "I think I know just the person to help us with this." Mistress Cavares. If there was anyone in Naru who knew how to translate archaic characters, she would.

Nikulo swallowed and drank from the spring. "Can you trust her? This is all Shadow and Poison Magic. You know it's banned by the Order."

He had a good point. Even though Mistress Cavares was considered eccentric to most wizards of the Order, she still adhered to its principles. And that included a strict forbidding of Shadow Magic.

"Maybe there is a way...without her seeing the Tandria Scroll."

Nikulo scrunched up his face and bent over like he had stomach pains. Talis stepped back, scared of what might happen. Toxic fumes. Nikulo waved a hand. "False alarm... So what's your idea?"

Talis led Nikulo to a side room in the temple where he often studied. A worktable contained hundreds of completed runes, blocks of clay, inscribers tools, and countless scrolls on Rune Magic. Nikulo picked up a scroll and frowned.

"What's all this?"

"Rune Magic."

Nikulo coughed. "Why are you spending your time learning this junk?"

Talis placed a rune—inscribed with the Praellic symbol for singing and one for a bird—on a chair next to the table. He cast a binding spell on the rune and it melted away.

"Go ahead, sit."

"What? Am I some kind of experiment?" Nikulo glanced suspiciously at the chair.

"Are you afraid of a little worthless rune spell?" Talis made a face daring Nikulo to try.

Nikulo frowned and placed a hand on the chair, then slowly sat. Soon, with fear spreading across his face, he started singing a horrific rendition of "The Barkeep's Plump Daughter" in a falsetto voice. Talis laughed as Nikulo's eyes got wider. Nikulo tried to put a hand to his mouth, but couldn't stop singing.

He finally finished, but by now Talis cried with laughter, rolling on the ground.

"You!" Nikulo shouted, his face red. "How could you do that? You're really lucky I'm a good singer...."

"You're a terrible singer!" Talis chuckled, shaking his head. "Don't ever try and become a bard. A comedian, yes, but never a bard."

"So the point of this is what? Runes can make people sing?"

"What's going on in here?" Mara said, peeking inside the room. "Was that a monkey dying?"

"Saved by the beautiful and charming Mara." Nikulo smiled and bowed low. "Talis has been giving a poor demonstration on the value of Rune Magic."

"Rune Magic?" Mara strode over to the table and inspected the clay tablets.

Talis told her about studying with Mistress Cavares, and Nikulo chimed in with the story about the Tandria Scroll. Mara's face darkened as Nikulo told the parts about Shadow Magic.

"So what mother has been saying about you is true? The black crystal is infecting your mind? Why are you studying dark magic?" Mara glared at Talis. "I thought you were a student of Light Magic?"

Nikulo put a hand on Mara's shoulder. "Talis isn't studying this… I only showed him the Tandria Scroll just now."

"Well then, why are *you* learning it?" She shook his hand off her shoulder and stepped back defensively.

"It's just what I do." Nikulo shrugged. "I used to be ashamed of studying Poison Magic, but since our trip…I feel it's okay. It's just another kind of magic. Right?"

Mara frowned and stared at the wooden shrine at the end of the room. "Like light and darkness, death and life… Just another—" She shook her head. "Now I'm all confused. I don't know…."

"What about this?" Talis took a pen, dipped it in an inkwell, and drew on a piece of vellum paper. "Here is light and here is darkness on the other side. Above could be poison and below could be healing energy. Maybe the reason why Nikulo is curious about Poison Magic is because it's the opposite of healing."

28

Nikulo nodded. "And the Shadow Magic portions of the Tandria Scroll, although I'm not interested in them, I thought Talis might find them of use, especially because you've master Light Magic."

"You do realize," Mara studied Talis, "that if you continue in the direction you're heading, you'll be declared an enemy of your own magical Order? Do you want that?"

"Not to mention Mara's parents," Nikulo said.

Talis scoffed. "They hate me already. Learning a forbidden art won't change that. But listen, this is different." He tapped the Tandria Scroll. "The knowledge within here can teach us how to cast portals! The Order can't teach us that—"

"They can teach us to fly."

"Master Jai refuses to teach me the spell. All the wizards shun me except Mistress Cavares and Master Grimelore. Even the Goddess Nacrea summoned a portal! If Shadow Magic can teach us that, and the Goddess uses similar magic, how can it be all bad?"

Mara looked unconvinced, so Talis tried a different approach. "Just imagine...we could go anywhere in the world we wanted... We could see each other without worrying who was watching us."

"I could get sweets in the middle of the night." Nikulo burped and reached for the last cake.

"Be serious!" Mara rolled her eyes. "Okay, I admit, casting portals would be amazing. If nothing but for not having to sneak around, that would be worthwhile. And speaking of which, I have to go back home before my parents discover I'm missing. Just do what you have to do…I won't judge you…until you start sprouting demon's horns. Then maybe I might have to kill you."

"Besides, who knows how long it will take us to figure out the portal spell?" Talis said.

Mara shrugged and said goodbye to them. "Might be awhile before I see you two… I'm sure I'll end up banned from leaving my house. Mother was furious when she found out we went hunting."

Talis waved at Mara as she left the temple, wondering if they really could master the portal spell. He glanced at the Tandria Scroll, recognizing a few of the characters similar to the runes. Maybe the answer *could* be found with Mistress Cavares after all.

4

Storm and Shadows

"There are many uses for runes beyond what I've taught you." Mistress Cavares studied Talis with her chilly blue eyes. "Tell me, what did you struggle with the most when you were first trying to do magic?"

Talis sighed, remembering all his failed attempts. "I was terrible...I couldn't do any magic for several years. In training dreams I could do it, but nowhere else."

"That's not uncommon. Students often fail at the mental concentration needed to bring the magic into focus...to produce for the first time. Often an emotional event is needed."

"When we were attacked by the Jiserians, that's when I first did magic."

Mistress Cavares nodded slowly, as if digesting his words. "Had you studied Rune Magic, you would have cast magic much sooner."

"Why is that?" Talis would have done anything at first to create magic. His first years studying at the Order of the Dawn were completely frustrating.

"With runes the magic is focused through the inscription and locked in with magical intent. Casting unaided magic is much more difficult. It's a miracle the Order produces as many wizards as we do—which is not enough—but still, we could produce even more with the aid of runes, especially for those apprentices that fail to cast straightaway."

If Talis was going to succeed in learning the portal spell, he knew he had to gain mastery over the languages needed for Rune Magic. And only Mistress Cavares could help him with that.

"Why are there no books to learn the ancient languages needed for runes?"

A wry smile crossed Mistress Cavares's face. "The danger is too great. The languages needed for runes can only be taught from master to student." She glanced at the rune Talis was inscribing. "I see you're learning your languages...quite an improvement. No, no, that's not the right combination. Second Kingdom with the Fourth Kingdom, fire and wind makes an inferno...yes, that's right."

How Talis learned languages from Mistress Cavares involved writing on sand and erasing the characters quickly. You either succeeded or failed the lesson. Talis had a doubly difficult task. The night before, he'd memorized all the characters from the first portal spell in the Tandria Scroll. He hoped Mistress Cavares would teach him a few of the characters so he could fill in the missing pieces.

"How would one go about creating a whirlwind?" Talis stared at her innocently. From the drawings on the Tandria

Scroll, he thought perhaps a portal might be drawn similarly to a whirlwind.

"A whirlwind..." Mistress Cavares tapped her head several times. "Have you studied Wind Magic?"

Talis shook his head.

"Good, good! I can teach you something new, and it will be with runes. Excellent." She drew four characters on the sand. Talis released his breath and smiled to himself. Three of characters were new, and he was pretty sure that those were the three missing characters he needed. Maybe they finally had a chance to master the portal spell.

"These two characters are from the First Kingdom, Velletrix. A strong wind and to churn with great force. These other two characters are from the Third Kingdom, Praellian. To strike and to propel forward. The combination of these four characters will create a rune of a specific nature, yet less powerful than a two-character rune. A good starting place for Wind Magic. Let me teach you."

She extended her palm towards a candle set along the wall. A burst of wind leapt out and consumed the flame. "Now you try it. Remember the last time you felt the wind striking your skin. Focus on the power flowing from your palm."

Talis pressed out his hand and concentrated on the feeling of the wind. The candle sputtered and wavered, but he failed to extinguish it.

"Try again. Practice until you can blow out the candle from across the room. And don't go creating a storm inside my workshop, either." She grinned at him.

After a half hour of practice, Talis had mastered the spell and could focus the wind on one spot, blowing out the candle in the process. Mistress Cavares nodded in approval after he succeeded several times.

"Shall we go for a walk outside the city and test our little rune?"

Talis found a devious smile spreading slowly across his face. A trip outside was just the thing he needed.

The forest outside the city was alive with wavering shadows. The wind had picked up, spreading rumors of a coming storm. Talis followed Mistress Cavares as she marched over boulders and fallen logs, her determination strong to find the right spot.

"This will do." Her gaze passed across a gentle meadow, protected by a stand of camphor trees.

"Should I place the rune here?"

"Not quite yet... First we need to prepare the stage. Can you go and gather four heavy sticks and several branches? We'll be building a trap."

Talis grinned as he bounded off towards the forest, searching for appropriate sticks to make a "trap." What did she mean by a trap anyways? Were they going to set the rune and try to catch an animal?

"Will these do?" Talis dragged four thick sticks and several leafy branches.

"Rather nicely…" Mistress Cavares glanced at him. "We're not trying to trap an animal, if that's what you're thinking. My vows prevent me from harming innocent creatures."

"Then what are we trapping?"

Mistress Cavares opened her mouth as if to speak, then closed it and smiled hideously. "You're trying to trick me…I see your game."

"Why would I do that? I simply want to know—"

"Build," she interrupted, "a four-sided trap, for the four directions, and cover three sides with the branches you've gathered. Leave the north-facing side open."

Talis grunted, but grabbed the sticks and started assembling a four-cornered pyramid. He tied the top with some vines, and placed the branches snug against the three sides. After he finished, he stood and inspected his work.

"Interesting construction…a pyramid." Mistress Cavares circled his creation, and bent down to peer inside. "Yes, this will work. Now place the rune in the absolute center of your trap… No, you'll need a stick to measure precisely. Go get one."

He could tell from her eyes that she was serious, so he held his sigh until he reached the forest's edge. Why did she always have to be so exact in everything? He thought this would be a fun outing in the swamplands, but instead it was just another one of her *lessons*.

But then he noticed something. From his vantage point he realized that the placement of the trap was also precise.

It was exactly in the center of the meadow. Now he was really curious. What was she up to?

When he found a stick straight enough to measure lengths, he raced back to the trap.

"That will do." Mistress Cavares motioned Talis towards his construction.

Talis measured the trap twice, trying his best to locate the center. "Can I place the rune now?"

Mistress Cavares wagged her head back and forth. "We must ask the wind first." She gazed at the sky, pressed her fingertips against her temples, and started chanting strange words in a staccato rhythm. Soon a dust-devil formed in the sky. The air smelled suddenly of spring blossoms and rain. The grey whirlwind moved slowly towards them, and finally settled over the trap.

The corners of Mistress Cavares's mouth curled up into a smile. "See? The wind listened to wisdom. And we, mortal servants of the gods, obey. Now you must sing praises to the gods."

"Sing?" Talis frowned, and glanced around as if expecting an audience. "Which gods?"

"All of them, foolish one. Do you want to make a god jealous? Start a war? Sing, boy, sing!"

Talis felt himself wither at her piercing stare. He cleared his throat and raised his eyes to the heavens. He remembered songs his mother had sung to him as a child, songs of love, songs of revenge, songs of the gods. His voice was clear and strong as he sang the words. He sang every song he knew, not missing any of the gods.

When he finished, a feeling of calm and strength possessed him. The storm had melted away and the meadow was strangely quiet. Shadows that had once belonged to trees on the forest's edge began stretching towards the trap from all corners. Talis stepped back in fear as the unnatural shadows moved closer and closer, bending in angles that defied the path of light. Defied the laws of nature. This couldn't be happening.

Mistress Cavares cackled softly as she stretched her hands towards the trap. Was she a dark sorcerer? Talis glanced nervously at the deep magenta mist forming in the air around her fingertips. Then swirls of that mist shot out in streams towards the empty nest of the trap he had built. An inky-blackness consumed the center of his construction, blacker moment by moment as the shadows poured inside.

The world was going insane. The trees around the meadow bent at odd angles, twisted and were made to bow low by some strange force. The trap glowed around the outside with that same magenta mist. Talis could hear a moaning sound like from the mouth of a slave bearing a crushing burden.

"Dare you venture forward and place the rune?" Mistress Cavares was standing as if she had lost all sight. Her eyes had flipped upwards so only the whites showed.

Talis wanted to run and leave this madness, but he didn't know if he could escape unharmed. The air sparked with electricity as if he was standing atop a hill being assaulted by lightning. The gods were here. Dark and light, trickster and healer.

"If you flee, the gods will slay you." Mistress Cavares stared at him with those hideous eyes.

"I will obey the gods." They came here for a purpose. Whatever this was must be an illusion. Would it fade away once he positioned the rune and cast the binding spell? So he strode forward and kneeled down in front of the trap, trying to avoid staring inside the blackness. When he put the rune inside, his hands disappeared. How could he see to properly position the rune? His fingertips could feel disease and rot and death.

"You must enter…use your power and find the right placement for the rune."

Talis glanced at Mistress Cavares, hoping to find something in her expression that might tell him this was all a horrible idea. But she was like the cold on a winter's morning. He turned back to the trap, and crawled inside, ignoring the feeling of terror slithering under his skin. The air was burning hot. As he fumbled around in the dark, his hands sensed a chill. He couldn't answer how he knew it, but this was the right spot.

He placed the rune and cast the spell. The rune flashed brilliant golden light, and sucked in the black mist. The characters inscribed on the rune shone for a moment, then the rune vaporized into ash and the trap collapsed around him.

"Quickly, retreat," Mistress Cavares said. Her eyes had gone back to normal, and her face now held a look of worry. "I may make a runemaster out of you yet…if this succeeds."

"But what was all that about?"

Mistress Cavares put a finger to her lips to quiet him. "We must wait for the thing that must come to arrive." She turned and led Talis over to duck behind an old, mossy log.

After many minutes of waiting, Talis heard the beating of hooves in the forest. A stag tall and proud. The animal pranced across the meadow. *Don't let it be this beautiful creature,* Talis prayed. The stag looked spooked and fearful. It darted around, then stopped and perked up its ears. A paw dug into the soft earth.

Shouts and the whinnying of horses and baying of hounds sent the stag bounding off into the opposite forest. Talis lifted himself up to see who it was, but Mistress Cavares held him back.

"Don't interfere with the hand of fate," she whispered.

"But what if someone is injured by the magical ward?"

Mistress Cavares raised an eyebrow. "Or much worse…" Talis glared at her, but she remained unaffected, and returned to stare across the meadow.

Soon the hounds came, slobbering and sniffing and barking in excitement. They caught the stag's scent and gave chase.

"Now comes the interesting part." Mistress Cavares chuckled.

Was she crazy? Talis glanced at the look of humor and bland determination in her eyes. She truly didn't care if someone died or was injured because of the rune he had cast. Well he cared. He stood, shaking off her hand from his arm, and ran towards the sound of horses galloping in the forest.

"Sit down, you fool!" shouted Mistress Cavares. "Would you rather save a human life or invoke the anger of the gods?" Her voice faded as Talis widened the distance between her and the hunters.

Three horses fled the forest and burst across the meadow. Another nearly ran Talis over despite his shouts and hand waving. The banners. They were the guardsmen of House Lei. Mara's family. Talis felt a cold sweat wash down his back. He had to warn them and keep them away from the magical ward.

"Get out of the way!" shouted a guardsman. He aimed his bow at Talis. "Can't you see we're on the hunt?"

"Over here!" Another guardsman on the edge of the opposite forest waved his banner. "The hounds have got the scent."

"There's danger here," Talis yelled, but the guardsmen had already bolted off towards the hounds.

The thundering of more hoofbeats sounded behind him. He whirled around just in time to duck. A massive destrier draped in purple silk leapt over him and landed directly in the path of the ward.

Talis shouted at the rider to stop but his voice was drowned out by the avalanche of war horses all around him. The destrier galloped defiantly into the center of the meadow, rider wielding a great horn bow. Talis raised his hands as if to cast a spell. What could he do to stop him?

But there was nothing to do. One second the destrier barreled forward, and the next a purple-black mist enveloped the rider and horse whole. Millions of shadow filaments exploded across the meadow, spreading like a flood of terrorized spiders.

5

Hunting Party

The man dressed in ornate leather armor catapulted from his destrier and shot into the air, his legs and arms flapping about. He slammed headfirst onto the unforgiving earth. If the body had been a doll, the head would have popped off. Instead a hideous *crack* echoed across the meadow, and cries were heard from the guardsmen circling their horses in confusion.

Talis wanted to move but found his legs were made of lead. His jaw dropped open, gaping at the wreck of a man splayed out, limbs twisted in impossible directions. The man's face remained untouched other than the look of utter shock in his eyes. Mara's uncle. Her father's youngest brother. Spoiled to the core, insolent and a black spot on the Lei family name. He'd made a habit of surrounding himself with brawlers, gamblers, liars, and cheats. Ralakh Lei's guardsmen now rushed to their master's body, fists pounding the earth. They grabbed their hair, and aimed curses at the gods.

Mistress Cavares's face was colorless as she stared at the broken figure. Did she still trust the fate of the gods? A cruel fate indeed. "This will not do," she mumbled.

"Not do?" Talis flared his arms in frustration. "A royal has been slain. At least I tried to warn him."

"*Warn?*" A guardsman's low, raspy voice spilled across the meadow. "Warn him of what?"

He was a giant brute of a man, and his eyes held a vile, murderous gleam that made Talis step back in fear.

"Don't...you don't understand." Talis glanced at Mistress Cavares for support but found none. "Can't you see I'm a royal? I'm Talis of House Storm...."

"You!" another guardsman shouted and marched up next to the first guardsman. This man had an enormous pot-belly from taking in too much ale and mutton. Pockmarks spread across his face like a bad tattoo.

The first guardsman stopped the pockmarked man. "I am Taige, first guardsman to Master Ralakh Lei. Until now." He glanced at the body. "I have failed my Master..."

Pock-Face leered at Talis. "This one...he's a troublemaker to young Mara. The Mistress of the House has forbidden Mara from seeing him and yet they still—"

"Cease your words. Talis Storm is famous in Naru...savior of our fine city." Taige spat on the ground in disgust. "Now answer my question!"

"You forget your station, *guardsman*. As a royal, I don't have to answer," Talis said.

"How do you fancy an accident out hunting?" Pock-Face said. "People get trampled by horses all the time. It would be such a pity."

"You forget about me...the witness." Mistress Cavares strode forward and raised a hand.

"Stand down, you old hag."

"Have you truly no fear of those wearing the robes of the Order?" Her fingers formed a bubble of black mist. Talis winced at the display of dark magic. How did she know this power?

"Sorcerer!" shouted a guardsman. "Traitor!" yelled another. The rest of the men, twenty or so, retreated at the display of magic.

"Return to your gambling dens and whorehouses." Mistress Cavares seemed to loom taller than her petite figure. "Or would you I rather turn you all into pigs and let you wallow in muck?"

Taige brandished a finger at Talis. "You will be called to answer for this, mark my words. There will be blood on the streets over this, young *master* of House Storm." He whistled and motioned the other men to help carry the broken body of Ralakh Lei. Talis felt a hard lump form in his stomach. How would he explain this to his family? Worse yet, how would he explain it to the Order?

Mara's face flashed in his mind's eye. Would she hate him over the death of her uncle?

After a long march back to Naru, Talis stared up at the four black flags hanging above the gates of Naru. He cringed as he recognized the expression of anger and disgust on the faces of the guardsmen at the entrance to the city. Mistress Cavares strode past him, bold and indignant despite the swarm of soldiers.

"You…Talis of House Storm, you've been summoned to House Lei!" yelled the captain of the guard. Talis recognized his helm's plumage as belonging to Mara's house guard.

"The young master will answer to no one but the Order." Mistress Cavares eyed the approaching captain and his men with a look that dared them to oppose her.

When her words did nothing to stop their charge, Talis thought about fleeing to the temple for protection. As the temple was far away to the north, he couldn't summon the massive power of the black crystal to aid him in a fight. He waited instead and watched as Mistress Cavares placed a rune on the ground and cast a binding spell.

"If you pass, you'll wish you never had a crazy idea like crossing a runemaster of the Order."

The captain raised a hand and ceased their march. He lowered his eyes to the spot on the ground where she had set the magical ward. "What treachery is this, witch? You'll burn for your use of dark arts."

Mistress Cavares cackled indignantly. "And now am I a *witch?* Thirty-five years in the Order, and never been treated so poorly." She lifted her eyebrows, and paused, surmising the crowd gathered around. "You puny blade wielders, holding steel as if it was actually dangerous to a wizard. Isn't it too *heavy* to carry such a weight around all day?"

When she had spoken the word "heavy," every guardsman wielding their blades sank to their knees in unison, faces pale and strained, and dropped their swords like it was the heaviest thing on earth.

"Now what weapon do you have left to wield?" Mistress Cavares laughed and covered her mouth shyly. "Men...all grown up but still boys."

Through the gate marched a unit of guardsmen flying the colors of House Storm. *Father's men*, thought Talis, feelings of hope and pride rising. Would they be able to keep this nightmare from turning far worse? He recognized Father's captain of the guard, Rallian, and waved.

"No one is to touch young Master Talis except his father's guard," shouted Rallian. "We're here to escort the boy home."

"Home?" yelled the captain of House Lei. "As this witch commanded, he must be taken to the Order. We will *help* escort him to the Order's chambers and see to it that no trickery happens."

Talis couldn't believe the feuding between the royal houses had gotten this bad. The air was bristling with the threat of violence. Mara's father would be furious. There would be blood on the streets tonight, and all because of Ralakh Lei's death and House Storm's involvement.

Mistress Cavares patted his shoulder. "Don't blame yourself, boy. I should have undone the spell once I heard horses." She sighed a heavy sigh. "It is hard to explain...the mood that possesses me after summoning the gods. The gods care little for ways of mortal men, and a good bit of that attitude can rub off on me when they have shown their presence. It's a merciless and cold feeling."

Talis understood little of what she was talking about, but nodded as if understanding anyways. She was strange, indeed. He locked his eyes on Rallian and marched forward through the crowd, allowing Father's men to envelop him. But he wasn't fooled for a moment that he was actually safe inside Naru. The only place he really felt safe was in the Temple of the Sun.

They marched through the lower city, the soldiers pushing their way through a crowd that had formed around the arena. Talis scanned around and spotted several instigators shouting curses at him. *Probably paid by House Lei to start a riot*, Talis thought. Rumors had swirled that Mara's father had eyes on the throne. King Balmarr Merillia remained silent. Everyone knew he was old and his mind was failing. The stress of the Jiserian siege had taken its toll.

As they left the tunnel to the upper part of Naru, children above tossed cabbages and tomatoes and onions onto the soldiers. An egg landed on Rallian's silver helm. He glanced angrily around the crowd as if he intended to maim the source of the attack. His eyes found nothing but a scattering group of vagabond boys.

He whistled and gestured for two lines of soldiers to push the crowd back and open up a pathway towards the Temple of the Dawn. The temple dome still remained broken, but many of the administrative buildings and teaching facilities were undamaged. Other deeper, secret chambers, including the Order's crypts and archives, were locked shut and guarded well.

"What have you done?" Master Viridian stood with an expression of contempt and disappointment on his face. "First you bring black magic into our midst, and now this?"

"It's not black magic—" Talis was interrupted by Master Viridian's raised hand.

"Enough talk here. Mistress Cavares, he is your pupil, lead him down to the Order's chambers. We will conduct our interrogation there. House Lei has brought formal charges against Talis." He frowned at her.

"They have provided credible witnesses."

"Credible?" Mistress Cavares scoffed. "Now those drunkards are credible in the eyes of the Order? My how the wind changes." She looked at Master Viridian with mistrustful eyes.

"They are members of House Lei, and Viceroy Lei vouches for them."

Master Jai of the Order motioned Talis inside. "This way, if you please."

When Talis arrived at the Order's chambers, he couldn't help but notice the lack of magical energy compared to the last time he'd visited. The air no longer crackled with power from the old temple crystal. Golden candles lined the stone interior of the vast, underground chamber. Comfort was not an option here. There were no seats or table like the Sej Elder's chambers. The far side of the room contained seven levels of ranking where wizards now stood and stared accusingly at Talis.

These were familiar faces, those Talis had fought with side by side in the battle against the Jiserians. He thought he still had allies here, but from the expression of suspicion and mistrust in their eyes, he knew all that was gone now.

Master Viridian ambled up the stairs to the top level and turned to address those gathered around the room. "We are here to judge the case of murder…murder against one of our own. Ralakh Lei was slain today by the power of dark magic." He jabbed the air with his finger pointing at Talis. "And this young royal and student of the Order is accused of this crime."

The crowd murmured and glanced around at each other and at Talis.

"Let me continue." Master Viridian raised a hand to settle the crowd. "Justice for this kind of heinous crime can be only one thing." He glanced at Talis with cold, doubtful eyes. Talis remembered Master Viridian's distant expression after he'd shown him the black crystal and wondered if that was the reason his old master was treating him like this.

When silence returned to the room, Master Viridian focused his gaze on Talis.

"The penalty if proven guilty is death…and we will not be lenient."

6

Dark Hand of the Gods

Talis felt himself shrink at his former Master's words. *The penalty is death...* From the time he was a boy, he'd always looked up to Master Viridian. He was the strongest and most powerful wizard in the Order, the only one able to cast Light Magic. That is until Talis had returned, armed with the power of the sun...and the power amplified by the black crystal. *He despises the black crystal and the Temple of the Sun,* thought Talis. But why did Master Viridian hate a temple for the Goddess Nacrea?

"Let all witnesses assembled before the Order hear the testimony of those sworn to defend and uphold the honor of Naru." Master Viridian stared solemnly at the House Lei guardsmen. Talis recognized them from the swampland. Would these men tell the truth? Talis glanced around, trying to spot a friendly face, and found his father pressing his way through the crowd.

"Talis, you must listen to me," Father whispered. "Speak the truth or they'll know, and tell everything that happened. I will be right here with the other Elders." Father gestured at the Sej Elders gathered to the right.

Talis cringed under Mara's father's glare, feeling his hatred ooze out from his eyes.

The scribe clapped his hands and called out for the first witness to stand and present. Master Vellar Lei raised his hand and pointed at Taige, first guard to Ralakh Lei, and the guardsman lumbered over to stand before the wizards. He raised his eyes to the wizards, his face tense and fearful.

"This young royal killed my master, killed him with a strange kind of dark magic." The room echoed with murmurs. "It was a trap I tell you."

"It was a trap," Mistress Cavares shouted and wove her way forward through the startled crowd. "A sanctified trap of the gods, created by myself. Who amongst the Order dares challenge the will of the gods? I bear witness that I myself crafted this trap, and summoned the gods... They heard and answered the call. Ralakh Lei was chosen to die by the gods themselves. If you are to blame anyone, blame me. I am his master of runes and teacher of ancient languages."

Cries of protest and surprised shouts raced through the crowd, and many lifted clenched fists at her in anger.

"I tried to warn him!" Talis said. "I didn't understand what it was all about. I never intended for the magical ward to kill anyone."

"Magical ward?" thundered Master Viridian. "You know how to place a magical ward?" He gazed in horror at Mistress Cavares. "You dared teach him this? I asked you to teach him runes and ancient languages. But traps and wards and summoning the gods? Don't you realize you've brought the dark hand of the gods upon us? Leave Zagros and the other dark gods hidden in the shadow realm!"

A loud, shrill hiss suddenly spread across the room and extinguished the candles all at once. The chamber was enveloped in pitch blackness. Terrified voices and shuffling feet told of the chaos all around.

Master Viridian illuminated the room with his hands beaming the radiance of Light Magic. His eyes were alert and flared open in alarm, scanning the room as if something horrible had arrived. Talis followed his gaze, noticing swirling clouds of darkness bubbling beneath the ceiling. What was happening?

"Begone darkness, begone dark gods!" Master Viridian shouted, beams of brilliant light shooting from his palms, attacking the dark clouds. "Let light fill this land and free our city from dark—"

But a barrage of lightning bolts amidst inky-black shadows struck Master Viridian in an instant. He cried out, his eyes flared open in terror. He moaned in pain as sickening jolts of electricity wracked his body in convulsions. Some hidden force lifted him off his esteemed position atop the seventh level, higher into the air, a burning, shining figure illuminating the dark chamber.

The vile smell of charred flesh stung Talis's nostrils and he turned his head away from the terrible sight. He couldn't believe this be happening, especially here in this sacred building....

"The gods! Appease the gods!" many wizards shouted in unison. Other wizards shrank back as more lightning bolts and shadow blasts slammed into those vocal wizards. Screams and shouts of terror ripped across the chamber.

Mass panic possessed the room, and the crowd quickly devolved into a riot. The wizards and guards shoved people aside, trying to flee the room, caring little about stamping on fallen ones. Talis backed to the wall and collapsed, unable to take his eyes off the scene. He fought back tears welling in his eyes and stifled a whimper as a burned and bloodied man shambled around the room, eyes glazed over. Then more cries of the dying and those in pain, shrieks and wails as the gods struck more wizards down.

Then the barrage ceased as if the sacred force had left the chamber. Talis could heard sobbing and moaning and pleas for help. Frightened of displeasing the gods, he kept quiet and stumbled over bodies littering the floor, wincing when flashes of light illuminated the wreck of charred and trampled bodies. He had to find his father.

Mistress Cavares came hobbling over, a look of shock and disbelief in her eyes. "Talis, you must leave this place quickly. I fear you'll only find refuge within the Temple of the Sun."

Talis shook his head, refusing to retreat. "We need to get help for the injured. I can't leave now…not after all this." He glanced around the room, and cupped his hand around his mouth. "Father! Where is he? I saw him just a moment ago…."

"Over here," Mistress Cavares said, and led him around the room to where the Elders had once stood. They stepped around a pile of bodies, a few still pleading for help. Talis recognized Mara's father, Viceroy Vellar Lei, cringing in the corner. The old man stiffened as he saw Talis, and raised himself up, jabbing a finger at Talis.

"You! You caused all this... Your meddling in the dark arts brought the displeasure of the g—" Elder Vellar glanced in fear at the ceiling for a moment, then turned and glowered at Talis. "I'll see you bleed for this. Guards, guards!" He scanned around as if expecting his men to arrest Talis, but none remained in the chamber.

"Talis," groaned Father, his voice was muffled from being underneath a pile of bodies.

Talis rushed over to where he'd heard Father. He carefully pulled aside an old, dead elder, and felt his heart drop as he saw his father's face panting heavily, eyes wide and panicked. How could they trample on their own people?

"Are you alright, Father?" Talis scanned his father for injuries, hoping he hadn't been struck by the gods.

"My leg... I think my leg is shattered." Father winced as Talis pulled a slain wizard off of him.

"It will mend...I'll ask the healer to tend to you. Thank the gods you're alive."

"My life is not important, Talis...but yours is. You must survive all this, you must keep the Storm family name alive."

"Guards!" shouted Elder Vellar, limping over to the entrance, casting angry eyes at Talis.

"You have to leave." Mistress Cavares clasped Talis's shoulder. "If you stay, I fear for your life…and the lives of others. We must avoid bloodshed between the Royal Houses. There's a way of escape over there, behind the fifth pillar…a crane's head…pull it and a tunnel will open for you."

"She's right," Father said, fixing his gaze on Talis. "This has gone too far in the wrong direction. You'll be safer in the temple."

"But what about you? What about the others?"

"I'll be fine. And as for the others…" He glanced around the wrecked chamber. "The gods have spoken their displeasure. Go now, son, go quickly."

Talis opened his mouth to object, but his father raised a hand to stop him. "You must survive, don't hesitate, go now!"

After he bowed hurriedly to his father and Mistress Cavares, Talis ran towards the fifth pillar. He could hear the marching of guards outside the chamber and the shouts of Elder Vellar Lei. The crane's head was old and resisted pulling, but Talis finally yanked it far enough out until a stone doorway opened. He dove inside and glanced around for a way to close it, and found another extended crane's head. He shoved it back in the wall and the door sealed shut.

Talis sighed and allowed himself to rest against the stone wall. What had just happened? Did the gods attack the Order, did they really kill Master Viridian? All because Master Viridian had tried to banish the darkness. The image of his old master's charred body flashed in Talis's mind. He found his heart racing as he leaned back, listening to the muffled sounds of soldiers' boots clacking against stone floors outside. This was the end of their peaceful city. Certainly House Storm and House Lei would be officially at war... And Mara, how would she take all this? Would he ever see her again?

The tunnel was completely dark and the air smelled of dust and rat droppings. Talis summoned a tiny amount of Light Magic, enough to faintly illuminate spiderwebs and rats scurrying down the tunnel. Where did the tunnel lead? Talis suspected it was built years ago to protect against the peoples' suspicion of magic. *Always have a way of escape*, Master Viridian had said. Talis couldn't believe he was really gone. His old master dead...slain by the gods. It was so sudden and unexpected. He thought of Zagros, Lord of the Underworld, and frowned, believing he was behind all this....

Why did Mistress Cavares have to create a trap and summon the gods? Maybe when the gods came they stayed around and followed Talis to Naru. Or maybe only the dark gods.

Talis reached a winding stone stairwell leading down and around, ancient runes engraved in each step. He must be somewhere near the massive walls of Naru on the north side of the city. The way had to lead outside. He thought he knew all the secret entrances, but here was one hidden right inside the Order. *The same Order that wanted to put him to death,* thought Talis.

At the bottom of the stairwell Talis followed a narrow corridor. Beams of late afternoon light stabbed the stone wall through slits. He was deep within the northern wall. He peered through one of the slits and gazed out over the vast Nalgoran Desert. The northlands, barren and cold, filled with memories of their expedition. He shuddered, picturing Rikar and Zagros and the Underworld, but forced himself to continue on.

He reached a dead end, with the only exit through a narrow archway leading to a ledge outside. Talis stared down. The cliff fell more than two hundred feet to the desert below. How was he supposed to escape? Off to the left, the Temple of the Sun shone under light piercing through the clouds. He could feel the magic of the black crystal from here. It was close enough for Talis to channel its power. But he doubted he could survive such a fall without knowing the flying spell that Master Jai had refused to teach him.

A sudden gust blasted Talis, pushing him back then pulling him dangerously close to the edge. His heart pounded and a chill prickled his skin. One more inch forward and he'd fall to his death. Or would he? Since Mistress Cavares had taught him to control the wind, could he use it as an ally and help soften his fall? Then an image flashed in his mind. The characters on the rune for slow fall. Even though he didn't have the rune with him, he was determined to try and write the characters on the ground and cast the binding spell anyways. A sudden thrill went through him. What if it worked?

He bent down and traced the characters on the sandy floor. Focusing his intent, he cast the binding spell over the symbols for slow and fall. Nothing happened. The wind picked up again and blew the stone floor clean. He sighed, and wracked his memory to recall any hint that Mistress Cavares might have given him in the past. Out of the corner of his eye the Temple of the Sun sparkled. Maybe if he drew from the power of the black crystal, the binding spell might be strong enough to work.

So he tried again, desperate to escape to a place of safety. He drew the characters, summoned the energy from the black crystal, and focused with all his willpower to cast the binding spell. The characters glowed faintly, shimmered, and disappeared. Did it work? Talis stepped onto the spot where he'd cast the binding, and felt a prickling along his feet and ankles. He jumped up, and sighed in relief as he fell slowly to the ground.

He glanced out again at the Nalgoran Desert. Fixing his eyes on the Temple, he steeled himself and leapt off the cliff.

Portal Spell

Talis didn't realize that by binding the spell to sand, the slow fall spell wouldn't last very long. He started plummeting fifty feet above ground, his stomach lurching up to his throat, and quickly thrust out his palms towards the ground and cast the wind spell Mistress Cavares had taught him. Twenty feet from mangling his body on protruding rocks at the base of the cliff, the wind spell caught purchase on the ground and pushed him up and away from the mountain. He cast the spell several more times until he finally landed and rolled on the soft sands of the Nalgoran Desert, his heart pounding in his chest.

He let out a sigh of relief, amazed he hadn't died, and looked up wonderingly at the towering cliff and walls. Had he really been crazy enough to jump from way up there? Thankfully he survived the fall, survived the insanity of the gods slaying most of the wizards of the Order, and he now wondered what lay ahead for him….

As he started for the green hillside capped with the Temple of the Sun, Charna, his pet lynx, padded over to greet him. She yowled like she knew something was amiss. Charna loved the Temple and spent most of her time sleeping in its shady corners, and hunting field mice and rabbits at night in the surrounding meadows. But when Talis came around she devoted herself entirely to him.

Tired and hungry, he wished he'd brought food. If only he'd kept more supplies at the Temple. But probably the only food around was what Charna hunted. No matter; if it came to that, he'd be forced to hunt for food as well. He had to stay close to the Temple for fear of arrest or attack from House Lei's guards or even by the Order itself. But no one would dare try to touch him here, with the power of the black crystal, would they?

Later on that night, after searching unsuccessfully for food in the temple, Talis climbed to the top of the Temple to his favorite spot with a clear view of the stars. He often slept here at night, bringing a blanket to ward off the evening cold. The Huntress, the Great Bear, the Treasure Box. The gods and mythological figures gleamed in the black sky. Were the dark gods pleased with all the mayhem they'd brought to Naru? He couldn't believe Master Viridian was really gone, and slain in such a horrific way. The night chill sank into his bones and sent a shiver through his body.

"Thank the gods, Talis...I prayed I'd find you safe here...." Mara hoisted herself up and over the wooden beam and ambled towards him, the air around her seemed tense and concerned.

"Mara! I can't believe you made it out of the city. It's all such a mess...such a sad and horrible day. Your father is furious with me. Are you angry at me…because of your uncle's death?"

"Ralakh Lei? He's was a drunkard and a glutton…I'm not surprised the gods chose him to die. No, I'm not angry at you, surprised yes, but not angry. I'm upset with my father, causing so much trouble, accusing you of killing my uncle. It was an accident, wasn't it?"

"Mistress Cavares was teaching me Rune Magic…out in the swamplands." Talis told her the story, shaking his head in disbelief. "I can't understand any of what's happened. Master Viridian dead? We've woken something into our midst, something better left alone…."

"The gods… But how could he die like that?"

Down in the Temple courtyard, Talis heard grunts and curses that sounded like Nikulo.

Talis stared down, and spotted Nikulo scratching Charna's chin. The lynx purred so loud Talis could hear it all the way up on the rooftop. "Need some help getting up?"

"I'd prefer you coming down. It's cold outside and I'm starving. My devout parents decided it was necessary to fast to appease the gods. The idea!"

Talis and Mara spidered their way down the Temple's beams, and jumped onto the courtyard. Nikulo's face held a pathetic grin like a sheep dog begging for his fair share of roasted mutton.

"I might have some food, but we'll need to hunt in the morning."

"Anything, really." Nikulo rubbed his now round and protruding belly. The rigors of the trip hadn't lasted long after he'd returned.

Talis stoked a fire at the hearth in the workroom, and rummaged around until he found some stale bread. Nikulo accepted the gift and crunched sloppily.

"All this sneaking about isn't going to work for long. You guys got lucky this time, probably because of all the confusion." Talis picked up a rune from the worktable. "We need to master the portal spell. Then we'll have the freedom to move around without anyone knowing."

"Did you have any luck with Mistress Cavares?" Nikulo swung his backpack around and withdrew the Tandria Scroll.

Talis nodded. "I have the missing characters, two from Velletrix, and one from Praellian."

Nikulo unfurled the Tandria Scroll. "How'd you manage that?"

"Powers of deduction and a bit of innocent trickery."

They peered over the scroll, and Talis tapped the illustrations of the portal. "Here, the Praellic character meaning *to lift*. Put them all together, and these are the four characters we need to cast the portal spell. *A strong wind and to churn with great force, and to lift and move forward.*"

"Shall we try?" Nikulo traced a finger over the characters.

Mara frowned. "Do you even know how to cast the spell?"

Nikulo stared at Talis. "I was hoping you had an idea… You're the one with the most elemental magic experience."

"Me?" Talis didn't have a clue, he expected that Nikulo knew because he'd already mastered the other spells of the Tandria Scroll.

"You're kidding, right?" Mara put her hands on her hips. "All this time and neither of you know? Don't you remember what Aurellia did when he cast the spell?"

"He just kind of raised his hands and the earth started sucking the temple inside the world's portal," Talis said.

"Aurellia's Elders cast preparation spells first," Nikulo said. "When Aurellia cast the spell, it looked like Light and Shadow Magic combined. At least that's what I thought."

"Same here. He did cast both at once." Talis glanced at the Tandria Scroll.

"Rune Magic." Mara pointed at a clay tablet.

"What?" Talis said.

"It's Rune Magic. The answer to casting the spell lies with the runes."

Nikulo raised an eyebrow. "Why do you say that?"

"Well, look at it this way." Mara studied Talis's face. "You said that with Rune Magic you need to inscribe characters onto a tablet, then you cast a binding spell. So inscribe these four characters onto a rune and try binding it. See what happens."

Talis laughed, feeling like an idiot for not thinking of it sooner. "And I'd just focus on the portal and where I'd like it to go when I cast the binding spell, right?"

Nikulo nodded. "Worth a try."

Talis selected a clay tablet, making sure it was of perfect proportions, and inscribed the four characters of the portal spell. He glanced at Mara and Nikulo, placed the tablet on the wood floor, and raised his hands to cast the binding spell.

As he closed his eyes, he tried to picture the swirling portal Aurellia had cast at the old Temple of the Sun. The mist and shadows and the light. A terrific agony took hold of Talis's heart: a feeling like Zagros, Lord of the Underworld, was staring at him with those cold, black eyes, but Talis also felt the sun warming his skin. Twin feelings, opposing forces. He combined those feelings with the image of the spring under the black oak tree outside the temple. It would be a safe test, and close enough in case anything went wrong.

When the magic flowed from his fingertips, Talis opened his eyes and watched silver and black energy pour into the rune characters. The rune evaporated into a dark cloud, and the spot where the rune once lay glowed a grey-silver ghost.

"Who wants to try?" Talis said.

Nikulo stepped towards the ward, pausing to inspect the ground. "If you don't mind, I'd like the honors since I discovered the spell in the scroll. And...where does the portal go, anyways?"

"Just outside the temple...I hope. We'll meet you there."

Talis gestured Nikulo towards the spot, and Nikulo swallowed in response, his face contorted into a grimace. If this worked, they could use the portal spell to transport to anyplace that they'd been before. Nikulo frowned and stared at the space on the ground where the magical ward was set, and hesitantly placed a foot there.

Hundreds of streams of silver and black mist swirled up and around from the ward, spinning and churning until a portal formed in the air. Thousands of miniature lightning bolts scintillated around the edges. They stared at the portal for a moment, feeling a chill seep through from the other side. Nikulo glanced back at them with a reckless expression, and jumped through the portal.

Talis and Mara locked eyes, grinned, and Talis took her hand and they ran outside the temple to see if it had worked. Talis spotted Nikulo flopped inside the spring, splashing water on himself as if he was taking a bath.

"Couldn't you have made the stupid portal go someplace else besides the spring?" Nikulo flapped his arms in the water and quacked like a duck.

Mara laughed freely, and glanced at Talis, who was unable to keep from chuckling at Nikulo.

"We did it, didn't we!" She flung herself around and gave Talis a warm hug. He couldn't help but notice she held him a bit longer than normal, and he found himself not wanting to leave. When they separated, Mara's face was flushed, and she quickly looked away to smile at Nikulo.

"I have to admit I had my doubts whether we could do it or not." Nikulo pushed himself up and stepped out of the spring, and wrung the water from his pants. "Now I'll never have to worry about food again…watch out cake shop, here I come!"

Mara chuckled. "Sure, let's use one of the most powerful spells in the world to resort to common food thievery." She poked his belly. "Your poor, ever hungry stomach will have to starve a little longer. I think you'd do well going on another adventure."

"As long as we can find taverns with ale, roasted pork, and apple tarts…you know the kind with fresh cream on top?" The sides of Nikulo's mouth glistened with drool.

"What do we do with him?" Talis lifted his shoulders and let his hands flop to his side. They'd succeeded casting the portal spell and it felt amazing, like they'd discovered the key to exploring the world…and maybe even other worlds. "But thanks to Nikulo and the Tandria Scroll we now know the how to cast portal spells!"

Nikulo spread his hands apart as if to indicate he was the greatest person on earth. "What can I say? I guess I am pretty awesome…."

Mara cleared her throat and smirked. "Somebody's head is about to explode with pride. Don't forget Talis, and I did help out as well. Anyways, well done. But the question is, what are we going to use the portal spell for?"

Talis opened his mouth to speak, thinking of ways to use the portal spell, but the vision of Rikar being tortured on that planet suddenly flashed in his mind. Why should Talis even think about helping him? After all he'd done to harm them and their city. Rikar had been a friend once, and he did help them along their journey, but still… Maybe Rikar was just unlucky and foolish enough to be tricked by Aurellia?

"What are you thinking about?" Mara brushed a strand of hair away from Talis's eyes, and he felt himself shiver in response.

The wind picked up from the north, a cold wind, smelling strangely of salt and the sea. Talis peered out over the Nalgoran Desert, dimly lit in the light of the four moon sisters. His skin prickled with chills, and he felt anxious about what was out there waiting for them. If the gods appeared so easily at the mention of them, and their anger so swift, then perhaps other ills were soon to fall over their city….

As Talis gazed across the meadows surrounding the temple and farther out to the desert beyond, a grey figure wobbled towards them in the dark, illuminated by the moonlight. A lone traveler, braving the northlands, and impossibly crossing the Nalgoran Desert on foot.

"Look over there." Talis pointed at the figure. Mara and Nikulo squinted, and shielded their eyes from the moons' glare.

"Where? I don't see anything," Mara said. "Wait, there it is, a shadow moving across the field. What is it?"

"Not a shadow, a figure." Talis strode forward to get a better look.

"I see a shadow as well, a rolling shadow," Nikulo said.

Talis concentrated, allowing the power of the black crystal to fill his body. He gazed at the location of the figure and closed his eyes. An old, leathered face appeared in his mind, curiosity and amusement pouring from pale-blue eyes. Those eyes, something hideously familiar, as if they reminded Talis of someone from the party in Darkov....

As Talis stared at the old man striding across the sands towards them, fire and wind and ice seemed to strike out from his eyes, and sent Talis tumbling dizzily to the ground.

8

An Unexpected Visitor

Talis pushed himself up, looking uncertainly at the old man who had suddenly appeared in front of them. He wore a black cowl that covered a scraggly mane of silver and black hair, and smelled of pine and lemon and salt. In his mouth he chewed a stick, and every now and then he rolled it around as he studied Talis, Mara, and Nikulo. Instead of shrinking back, Talis stood his ground, feeling a strange familiarity with the traveler.

"I am aware of a certain young wizard from the lands of the south." The old man's nostrils pulled in as he inhaled a deep breath of air. "And I find myself in a precarious predicament. I don't like situations I can't control." His hands flung out wide, startling Talis. "I'm used to a kind of...dominance, a certainty that allows me to prevail in all things."

The traveler took a hesitant step towards Talis, keeping his eyes low. He glanced up quickly at Talis. "Do you grasp my meaning?"

Talis flushed with irritation, then composed himself when he thought how it might apply to himself. "Actually...I suppose I do know what you mean. I too am used to dominating...." His voice trailed off as he glanced at the Temple of the Sun.

"You see, the problem with most sages is that they have too much knowledge and too little imagination." The old man cleared his voice. "Day is day, and night is black. And...*bad things* lurk behind the curtain of night. Don't they now?"

"The stars shine beautifully at night." Mara lifted her eyes to the sky.

The traveler tilted his head, as if considering her words. "Or the fury of the black universe chokes the stars into submission, until only a meager portion of their brilliance shines through. Which is it?"

"Neither," Talis said. "Half-truths for halfwits."

"Hah! Oh, I like this young wizard, truly I do. Ahhh, at long last I can rest these weary feet and enjoy fine wine, roasted...oh, what is it you hunt around here?" The old man flung aside his animal-skin backpack, and let it thump to the ground.

"Deer, quail, boar, if you're good." Mara grinned at the old man.

"Boar...how I long for the taste of roasted boar and red wine."

"Ahem, we seem to have the problem of not possessing said game and wine." Nikulo rubbed his stomach. "I don't recall ever trying to hunt in the dark."

"Hunt indeed!" the traveler interrupted. "A fine idea, my boy. Fine *indeed*." He glanced around the air liked he'd spotted moths fluttering about in the night. Quick as a falcon, he grabbed something from nowhere, and pulled out a long spear. Talis choked back his surprise, and coughed.

"Here we are, a mighty fine spear to go hunting with, don't you agree?" Then the old man stumbled forward, like a drunk or a man possessed by demons, and aimed his spear at the ground like he was hunting for snakes.

He jumped back suddenly, as if startled by something approaching. "There, there! Can't you see how magnificent he is? What a specimen. You don't see many like that these days... A real prize-winner, he is." If it weren't for the fact the man was obviously a sorcerer, pulling spears out of thin air and talking in riddles, Talis would probably have judged the man mad.

"Move out of the way! Here he comes," the old man shouted. He took several confident steps backward, and deftly threw the spear at the place where he'd been staring all along. Just when Talis thought the spear would fall onto the earth, brilliant white tusks and a massive boar's head appeared from a kind of blur in the air, and met the full force of the spear as it penetrated at the crown of the creature's chest. A direct strike. The creature squealed in pain, and writhed around with the spear still stuck inside its body.

The boar toppled over, panting last breaths, eyes open in fury.

"I had no idea you've such fine game here in the south! To think I've spent all these long years on Tarasen and never ventured to your city before..." He withdrew the spear from the boar's chest, and let it slide down into the sleeve of his robe where it disappeared. Talis found himself gaping at the old man's feats of magic, so strange and unconventional. No one at the Order had performed such magic, it would've been deemed low and useless, like common street performers and court jesters.

"You're from the Tarasen Isles?" Talis jutted his chin towards the man.

The traveler covered his mouth and coughed slightly. "I *rule* the Tarasen Isles. Much like you rule the land surrounding this fine Temple of the Sun." He shifted his head towards Talis. "Thanks to the immense power of the crystal planted directly underneath our feet."

Talis took a step back defensively, and had to force himself to keep his hands lowered. But he stared at the old man, refusing to let his concentration waver.

"You may relax, young wizard...I'm no threat to you, especially not here on your stronghold. I've merely come to pay my respects and to see you and this fine temple with these old, tired eyes. I've been rude...please allow me to introduce myself, I am called Palarian by those close to me. To the inhabitants of Tarasen, they know me as The Shelterer, the protector of their lands. Kind and cruel master of Tarasen." Palarian took a low, elaborate bow. "At your service."

"Welcome... It seems you know much about the temple and about me." Talis glanced at the man hesitantly. "You've traveled a great distance to visit Naru. As you said, food and drink is in order. The food"—Talis gestured at the boar—"you've provided, as to the drink, all I have to offer is water from the Temple's spring, which is fine, I can assure you."

Palarian sauntered over to the fountain where the spring bubbled up, and cupped several drinks. He sighed, his face expressing delight from the taste.

"Indeed, you're quite right. A magical spring. I feel rejuvenated already. Shall we roast this fine creature?" His fingers snapped and red-hot coals and fire appeared on the ground near the boar. He mumbled a few words and an iron roasting spit appeared over the coals.

"There, that will do nicely. I always loved the idea of hunting, but hated the messy parts of preparing the roast. Perhaps that's why I turned to magic at a very early age?" His fingers formed an edge, and a brilliant skinning knife appeared near the boar. His other hand raised, and the boar lifted into the air. The magical knife made quick work preparing the boar for roast.

"How did you learn such a thing?" Mara said, her mouth gaped in fascination.

The sorcerer chuckled. "I've had years of practice..." He commanded the boar to move and connected it with the spit roast iron. "Now, the special lathering oil my grandmother taught me: garlic and black truffle infused olive oil soaked in rosemary springs."

Nikulo literally drooled as the low flames from the coal sizzled after the oil had splattered off the boar. The air smelled hideously rich as the boar roasted. "And the wine, kind sir? You mentioned a *good* red wine. We wouldn't want to disrespect this fine boar with anything less, would we?"

"Ah, yes, the wine." Palarian scratched his silver and black mangy beard. "I've had wines from all over the world, and I have to say I'm partial to *Jiserian* vintages from the south."

Talis, Mara, and Nikulo went silent, staring at the sorcerer like he was a viper. Were the Tarasen Isles allied with the Jiserian Empire, their enemies? Was this sorcerer sent here to challenge Talis in a duel?

"I see I've struck a sensitive chord with the young masters. The war still not over yet?" Palarian flicked his wrist and the boar circled around on the roasting iron, pops and crackles of oil on the fire sending out a smell that made Talis ravenous with hunger.

"Please, sit by the fire. The roast will be ready soon." The old man reached into his robes, and withdrew a bottle of red wine. "The finest vintage in Carvina, stolen from the Jiserian emperor's own cellars."

Palarian's eyes sparkled devilishly. "Now how about that drink?"

Talis released a sigh, and sat, warming his hands by the fire. "Anyone who steals from our enemies is a friend of Naru. I'd be happy to share a drink with you, traveler."

The sorcerer pulled a crystal goblet from the other sleeve, popped the cork, and poured a glass of velvety-smooth red wine that wafted aromas of cherry and oak and honey into Talis's nostrils.

"There, now, and a glass for the young lady, and for the young gentleman…."

"I'm usually called worse things," Nikulo said, and grunted. "But I'll gladly take your wine, and a cup or three more." He took the goblet and raised it in toast to the others. "To new friends and old enemies, may our friendship bloom and our enemy's arses wither." Nikulo downed the full glass, and tried stifling a belch, but it came out as a rumble instead.

Palarian let out a small laugh. "Colorful friends you have, young wizard. This one has the gift as well?"

"Healing." Talis took a sip of the wine, and let the smooth liquid roll around in his mouth. "And other *useful* magic."

Nikulo squinted in appreciation. "And you, traveler? What's your story? All this way to simply pay your respects?"

The corner of the sorcerer's mouth raised in a half smile, and to Talis's eyes, the expression of deception. "Word has spread across the world of your power, young wizard. The boy who holds the magic of the Goddess

Nacrea in his hands. And of course, of the new Temple of the Sun."

"Along with the black crystal." Talis studied Palarian for any hints, but the sorcerer's face remained unmoved.

"A rare power indeed flows here from the earth, bringing life-nurturing energy to the land surrounding the temple." The sorcerer closed his eyes and inhaled a long, noisy breath through his teeth. "I can feel its power flowing through me... I do not wither, nor die, it nurtures me too, as you."

Talis frowned. Could Palarian channel the magic of the black crystal? Was there danger of losing the temple and its power to this stranger? He took another sip, and searched the old man's eyes. No, if he intended to fight and control the temple he'd have done so awhile ago, if he could even command the crystal's power. Talis always had a feeling that the black crystal was alive and sensed those drawing from its source. The sorcerer was unknown to the crystal.

"Eat, eat, what are we waiting for? I know I'm famished and you appear starving as well, especially the young master with the hungry belly." Palarian grinned at Nikulo. He flicked his fingers and the knife appeared once more and began carving the roast. The sorcerer pulled a fine silver platter from a misty shadow, and positioned it underneath the magical knife.

Nikulo scrambled forward to get his portion, nearly knocking Mara aside in the process. He shoved a slice into his mouth, closed his eyes, and chewed with a look of complete satisfaction.

"How is it that the roast is ready so soon?" Mara inspected a slice of the meat.

"Fire Magic," Talis said. "There's knowledge of sending controlled amounts within a creature."

The sorcerer raised an eyebrow at Talis. "This is known here in Naru?"

Talis nodded. "By one master, and now by his apprentice."

"I see. Such a rare wizard well-versed in a wide set of knowledge. And from the rumors surrounding your deeds, have gained mastery over at least one of the greater arts." Palarian placed the platter filled with slices of boar on the earth between them, and motioned them to eat.

But the sorcerer didn't eat, his mind appeared lost in thought as he stared at the fire. "There's something unsettled here in your fair city, and I can't quite place it. Something is wrong? The hero of Naru away from his family, alone with his friends, and hungry." He peered into Talis's eyes. "Yes…yes, something has gone wrong. The prophetess did not foresee lies. She glimpsed truth in her vapor-induced visions. *The hero cast aside from the ones he saved. The child of the sun plays with shadows. The gods strike fear amidst believers.*" Talis felt a chill run down his spine at his words.

Palarian released a long, tired sigh that caused his wrinkled, sun-worn face to appear hundreds of years old. "There's only one thing to be done, you know. The ancient sages spoke of this thousands of years ago. Mastery over the power of the sun must be followed by mastery over shadows. Otherwise unbalance occurs, and the mind bends and distorts and becomes unstable."

He leaned over and pierced the earth with his finger, and drew the ancient symbol for darkness.

"You must learn Shadow Magic."

9

Ancient Knowledge

Talis felt like a mallet had slammed into his stomach. His hands dropped to his lap, and he stared at the fire. A flutter of pops and crackles launched from the coals, sending a shower of sparks into the air. Mara was right, he'd taken dangerous steps on the path to learning forbidden magic, and now, the sorcerer was telling him he had to go even farther? Would it take him away from his family and city, the very things he'd fought so hard to protect?

"And you plan to teach me Shadow Magic?" Talis smirked as he stared at the sorcerer.

Palarian found a stick, broke it and tossed it into the fire. "Ah, but you misunderstand me. I lack the knowledge of the dark arts."

"You what?" Talis said. Mara and Nikulo stared at each other with a puzzled look on their faces.

"I believe you heard me just fine. I cannot teach you Shadow Magic." The sorcerer curled his fingers together and blew smoke rings into the air. "However, I do possess certain information that could guide you in your quest to gain a deeper understanding of dark magic."

"But why should I try to learn Shadow Magic?" If Palarian lacked the knowledge of Shadow Magic, who would be there to guide him if things went wrong? Talis remembered all his failed attempts at Fire Magic, and how Master Viridian had patiently guided him in his training dreams.

The sorcerer frowned at Talis, as if he was watching a patient slowly die. "You'll go mad... Why do you think the Goddess Nacrea gave you the black crystal? Think about it. She wanted you to learn dark magic to balance out the burning force of Light Magic. Just as the ancients have done for thousands of years."

Palarian stood, and brushed off his robe. "And not only the ancients knew this...but here within your very city, deep in the locked and barred subterranean passages of the Order of the Dawn, lies the knowledge of Shadow Magic."

"Within the Order, you say?" Nikulo's face held an incredulous expression.

"Yes, indeed, hidden away for centuries, available only to a select few wizards."

"And how do you know all this?" Talis said.

"While I may lack the actual knowledge of these dark arts, I do possess knowledge of worldly going ons through my vast experience here on this world. I've watched the rise and fall of kingdoms, the movement of scrolls, sages, wizards, sorcerers, and mystics over the years. Starting from the source, on that ancient island, Lorello: the twin cities of Urgar and Darkov. The fall of that great city of light, and the diaspora of knowledge throughout the world."

Palarian sighed, and ran his spindly fingers through his hair. "Yes, I've been one of the Watchers. Watching and waiting over thousands of years." Was this man one of the ancients?

"Waiting for what?" Mara ran a finger along the rim of her wine goblet.

The sorcerer's eyebrows flicked up and down in amusement, and he wagged a finger at her. "What's important is how do we get inside the Order's archives? If you're to learn Shadow Magic, that's the only place for you to start...unless you plan on sneaking into the Jiserian Empire. The Order of Shadows in the magnificent City of Corvina contains a wonderful collection of scrolls on the dark arts. But I'm guessing you'd have an impossible time getting inside, let alone figuring out how to translate the secret code the scrolls are written in."

Talis pictured the Order's archives, filled with dust and scrolls and clay tablets. Since the destruction of the Temple of the Order of the Dawn, the Order had forbidden entry to the library. But now, in the confusion since the incident with the gods, perhaps the archives would be unguarded?

"And will Talis truly go mad if he fails to study Shadow Magic?" Mara said.

A grave expression came over Palarian's face. "Sadly, yes. I've seen firsthand the insanity strike a fellow magician. A boy, a few years older than Talis, his name was Fineas, if

I remember correctly. He'd mastered Light Magic and was forced to use it to defend his Order against a rival group of sorcerers. The exertion drove his mind too far in one direction, and caused him to go mad, each day worse than the one before. There was a plan to teach him the dark arts to balance the force of light, but the only sorcerer in the Order with the knowledge of Shadow Magic had been slain."

"That's terrible!" Mara's eyes were tensed and worried listening to the story. "What happened to him?"

"He ended up going over to the side of his enemies, to learn Shadow Magic, and turned traitor. Most likely the dark arts compelled him unconsciously in that direction. He remained quite mad throughout his life, and was eventually slain by his former Master."

Talis shuddered, thinking of the fate that had befallen Master Viridian. "I'll do it. Let's sneak inside the archives."

"Are you sure?" Mara said, placing a hand on his arm.

"We have no choice. Besides, I've been meaning to visit the Temple archives." After all this time studying runes with Mistress Cavares, he needed to fill in a few gaps in her teaching. Talis glanced at Palarian. The question was, did he trust the sorcerer to come with them?

The old man seemed to read Talis's expression, because a grin spread over his face. "I know, you don't want me to come. Go ahead, but you don't really know what you're looking for. You need a guide."

"How do we know you're not going to sabotage the archives, and try and steal something you need?" The wind gusted up and sent the sorcerer's hair twirling. Talis put a hand behind his neck and studied the old man's face.

"You don't know." Palarian shrugged and suppressed a yawn. "I suppose I could give you my word."

"And how do we known your word even means anything?" Mara said.

"Well, there's a way to bind one's word to magic, a harmful spell for instance would strike, if you break your word." The sorcerer pushed out his lower lip thoughtfully. "Do any of you know the art of runes?"

Talis felt his heartbeat thump ahead erratically. He tried to keep his face stony, but the sorcerer picked up on something.

"So, you do know the hidden art. Rare, very rare to see in wizards these days. There was a time, quite a long time ago actually, when Rune Magic was all the rage. Now you'd be hard-pressed to find a runemaster in a kingdom." Palarian sighed, and rubbed the back of his hand across his lips. "I've learned a thing or two about runes over the years...."

"Follow me." Talis grunted, and led the sorcerer inside the Temple, summoning an orb of Light Magic to guide their way. If the old man had something to teach him concerning the use of runes, he was more than happy to learn. Shadows sprung to life as Talis sent fingerlings of flame to light the many candles scattered around the workroom.

Palarian's eyes went wide as he caught sight of all the runes spread across the worktable. He lifted a rune too quickly for Talis to stop him. "So much for worrying about how we'll get inside the archives. You surprise me boy, you do. Who taught you the portal spell?"

"Err, no one exactly taught me, we"—Talis gestured to Mara and Nikulo—"sort of figured it out."

"You did most of the work." Mara sauntered up alongside Talis, until he felt her hand brush lightly against his wrist, sending a shiver up his arm.

"Let's just say we solved a puzzle." There was no way Talis was going to tell this stranger a thing about his interactions with Aurellia. Palarian knew too much about him already.

"I suppose that's good enough." The sorcerer crinkled up his forehead and frowned. "Since you can open a portal, and I assume you've been inside the archives before, we should be ready to go."

"You forgot something..." Talis pointed at a rune with a Fire Magic spell inscribed. A quite specific spell afflicting one's internal organs. Like a kidney roast. "Teach me how to bind your word to that rune. If you break your promise...."

"I wouldn't want that to happen." The sorcerer rubbed his stomach, an unpleasant expression lingering on his face. "The binding is quite similar to any other rune binding, except I say my words of promise, and you bind them through your intent to the rune. Easy enough?"

Talis nodded uncertainly. "I'll give it a try." He placed the rune on a chair, and closed his eyes, waiting for the old man.

"I, Palarian, do humbly swear before the gods old and new, roaming the skies and ruling the deep, that I will bring no harm to the Order of the Dawn temple archives, nor steal, nor bring any ill deed to the archives. If I do, may the spell inscribed on this rune strike me down."

At the completion of the old man's words, Talis focused his mind on the binding spell, drawing the sorcerer's intent foremost to his thoughts, and pushed them inside the rune tablet. He opened his eyes just as the rune dissolved into dust, and left a shimmering silver ghost atop the chair.

"Could we perhaps test it on a mouse first?" The sorcerer shrank back a bit as he stared nervously at the chair.

"How could you even *think* of doing something to harm a poor innocent mouse." Mara scowled at him.

Palarian glanced left and right, as if searching for an escape. "I suppose you know what you're doing?"

"Not really." Talis stared blankly, remembering he'd just cast his first rune binding a few days ago.

"You're not inspiring much confidence." The old man ran his fingers along the top of the chair, and pulled it around. "Glass of wine to pair with my roasting?"

Nikulo chuckled, and filled his glass. Palarian gulped down the red liquid and exhaled. "Here goes...."

His face paled as he sat, the chair croaked in response. Nothing happened, at least from what Talis could see on the outside. The sorcerer cleared his throat, flashed a quick nervous smile, and stood.

"Well, then, it appears you've done at least one thing right in your casting. Shall we proceed to the portal spell? I'm fed and slightly drunk and ready for adventure."

Talis took the portal rune from the old man's hand. He also grabbed a few extra runes laying on the table he'd crafted before. Near the edge of the workroom, he positioned the portal rune on the floor.

"Before you cast," Nikulo said, "consider one thing. The Order of the Dawn is in a bit of a mess now, and any interaction with them would be perilous. Tread carefully inside. I don't want to fight my fellows at the Order."

Talis agreed, especially after all that had happened. "We should be very quiet inside."

"I know of something better. Better to go in unseen and unheard, don't you agree?" Palarian brushed his fingers against each other and mumbled to himself. "Who is first?"

Mara frowned. "You're going to make us invisible?"

"Precisely. Are you ready, my dear?" Palarian aimed his fingers at her.

"Wait, let me go first," Talis said.

"You don't need to be so chivalrous," Mara said. "Ladies first, after all."

The sorcerer nodded, and flicked his wrists. Mara vanished.

"Did something happen?" she said.

"I can hear you but not see you." Nikulo reached out to the space where Mara once stood.   "Hey, don't touch me there, you pervert." Talis heard a slap, and the back of Nikulo's hand went red.

Talis chuckled as Nikulo blushed. "I didn't mean to do anything, really."

"Liar." Mara started giggling.

"Will we be able to see each other when we're all invisible?" Talis said.

"Yes, of course. But others unaffected by the spell will not."

Talis spun around as something tickled the back of his neck. The next moment someone pushed behind his knees, and he started tumbling down. But just as he fell, he caught that someone's wrist (he knew it was Mara), and she landed on top of him.

"Cute, Mara." He could feel her squirming on top on him, but he held her with one arm, and tickled her with the other.

"Stop it!" she gasped, and squirmed even more, squealing and shrieking the more he tickled. Talis couldn't help but notice that she only slightly tried to resist him. It was almost like she enjoyed staying put where she was.

Palarian cleared his throat. "Perhaps we continue now? Are you next, young master?" He flicked a finger at Nikulo, and he disappeared in a vaporish flash. "Cast the portal spell, if you're finished tickling her."

As Talis rose, he let his hand slide down her arm until he grasped Mara's hand, and lifted her up. He spun around and faced the rune setting on the floor. He closed his eyes, pictured a favorite corner in the archives, and cast the spell.

The swirling silver and black portal sprung to life in front of him, a dark eye inviting them inside. The sorcerer flicked his wrists at Talis and himself, and Mara and Nikulo reappeared, ghostly this time, as the world went grey. The sorcerer raised his hands towards them.

"One last spell, so others won't be able to hear us, but we'll be able to talk amongst ourselves." He cast the spell and it was done.

Talis motioned Palarian and Nikulo towards the portal. Mara clasped hands with Talis, and pulled him through.

10

The Dark Archives

Instead of finding the archives dark and cold, as one would expect at this late hour, they discovered the chamber illuminated by a pale-blue magical light, and filled with the low murmurs of voices deep in conversation. Talis held his breath for fear of being discovered. Mara pulled him over to where Nikulo and the sorcerer stood against a wall lined with paintings of dour-faced wizards from years past.

"They can't hear us," Mara said. "You can breathe now."

Palarian nodded in agreement, and pointed towards a gathering of wizards from the Order. Talis recognized Master Jai, Master Grimelore, Mistress Cavares, and several other older members he had seen from the assembly earlier that day.

"We must tread carefully, a cautious approach in dealing with the boy will yield us the best results." Master Grimelore clapped his hands together, startling Talis.

"I disagree," Master Jai said. "I've seen the boy in action and it's a terrible sight to see. If we don't act decisively, I fear disaster will once again strike our city… Perhaps they will lash out again?"

He lowered his voice at the word "they." Talis thought maybe he was referring to the gods. Were they talking about attacking him directly at the temple?

Mistress Cavares cackled softly. "You're a fool. You think you're a match against the power of the black crystal? You feel confident of your new found dark power... Yet what you fail to realize is that the boy possesses mastery over a greater art, which you lack. And he's on the road to discovering another, thanks to my little lesson out in the swamplands. Quite unfortunate that House Lei decided to pursue an unannounced hunting expedition in the same area. Poor Ralakh Lei. Couldn't have happened to a more suitable pompous ass."

"Be wary of your choice of words, Mistress Cavares." Master Grimelore frowned. "These walls have ears." The other wizards nodded, and narrowed their eyes at her. "You understand that with Master Viridian and many of the wizards gone, House Lei will most likely impose its will on the city."

Talis wanted to protest, but kept himself calm. House Lei ruling Naru? Why would the king and House Storm ever allow it?

"Yes, indeed. With the king ill over the news of Master Viridian's death, the shock is taking its toll on the king's already weak heart. And there are rumors that House Lei is preventing the healers from doing their proper work on the king."

"What!" Mara said, and curled her fingers in anger. Talis looped his arms around her waist to keep her back.

Palarian put a finger to his lips. "Be calm, child," he whispered. "The magic subdues sound greatly, but I imagine these sensitive wizards can feel waves of emotions around them."

Talis knew it to be true. He'd seen Master Jai sense anger, intentions of violence, and lies. Out of the corner of his eye, Talis swore he glimpsed Mistress Cavares glance over in their direction. But then she turned back to the other wizards and continued talking about what to do now that the Order was weakened.

After a few minutes, the wizards of the Order finished talking and left the room, the pale-blue magical light following them out until the chamber went dark. Talis could hear Mara breathe softly next to him, but other than the ghost images of the wizards talking moments before, he couldn't see a thing.

"Do you think they all left?" Mara said, and placed a hand on his back.

"We'll need to see without creating light," Palarian whispered. It sounded like the sorcerer rubbed his fingers together, and the next moment the room was visible in a kind of ghostly grey and silver light.

"Much better... Where did you learn all those spells?" Talis glanced at the old man.

"Oh, I've have years to pick up bits and pieces here and there from very talented wizards and mystics of all kinds."

"Yet you don't know Light Magic or Shadow Magic?"

The sorcerer furrowed his brow, and averted his eyes from Talis. "I've never been inclined to learn either art. Let's just keep it at that, shall we?"

Something was odd in the tone of Palarian's voice, but Talis didn't push the sorcerer further. He followed the old man into another chamber, down a stone spiral staircase, and into the vast expanse of the main collections chamber. Piles of vellum scrolls were stuffed into wooden cubbies filling an entire wall from floor to ceiling twenty feet up.

"How is it you know your way around the archives so well?" Talis wondered who Palarian was and what he really wanted....

Palarian sniffed. "I arranged to meet the master builder who designed much of Naru, including the archives. He was most gracious to lend me a copy of the blueprints." The way the sorcerer said this made it sound like the master builder had no choice in the matter.

The old man trudged down a long narrow corridor, to an area of the archives off-limits to Order apprentices. The way split left and right, but the sorcerer lifted a wooden trapdoor, and ducked down inside another staircase. This was all new to Talis. He'd heard there were many hidden and locked chambers within the archives, but they'd been warned by the Masters to avoid even thinking of what might lie within. Not that that had stopped Talis from being curious.

Mara placed her hand on Talis's shoulder as they descended the steep stairwell, stone steps placed irregularly as if to trip unfamiliar feet. They wound their way left and right, straight, and curved left again until they finally reached the bottom, following the sorcerer down another narrow stone corridor.

They reached a dead end.

"What do we do now?" Mara said, peeking around Talis.

Palarian remained quiet for a moment, as if lost in thoughts. "This wasn't in the blueprints."

"The Masters probably changed it after the builder left Naru," Talis said. "Be careful about touching anything." Since Talis had learned about magical wards, he suspected their use by the founders of the Order of the Dawn. Or even more recently, by Mistress Cavares....

"You might have warned me before we went down here." The sorcerer's voice held a tinge of fear. He stared down the corridor behind Talis.

"What is it?" Mara glanced back, following Talis as he turned around.

"We're extremely vulnerable down here," Nikulo said, twisting around uncomfortably. "What exactly are we looking for, anyways?"

"The Dark Archives..." Palarian raised his hands, still staring down the corridor where they'd come from. "So why shouldn't have I touched anything?"

"Magical wards...I'm guessing one of the wizards might have set them, as traps or to warn of intruders. If this is a forbidden area, that's what I'd do." And Talis guessed that's what Mistress Cavares would do as well.

"If someone comes down here they'll find us...it's too narrow." Mara squeezed herself against the wall.

"How long would it take before they'd arrive?" The sorcerer's hands trembled as he aimed them down the corridor.

"Ten, maybe fifteen minutes at the most."

They waited in silence, staring down the corridor and listening for any hint of movement. But no one came after what seemed like an hour.

"Safe?" Mara said, and glanced up at Talis.

He nodded, and turned back to the dead end. "Search for any levers or loose stones."

"I doubt they'd make it that easy." Palarian searched the stone wall. Talis joined in, but the surface revealed nothing. Mara and Nikulo found nothing either after minutes of searching.

"So what do we do now?" Mara said.

"I wish I could say I had a spell to aid in this, but I can't think of anything." The sorcerer frowned at the wall. "Any direct elemental assault would most likely be guarded by magic."

Talis had an idea. "Whatever is down here was probably only accessible by Master Viridian, and maybe only one other wizard as backup."

"Why do you say that?" Nikulo said.

"Who are the two wizards in the Order that possess the only knowledge that none other in Naru have? Master Viridian knew Light Magic, and Mistress Cavares knows Rune Magic. May I?" Talis gestured towards the dead end. Palarian and Mara moved aside, allowing him to pass.

"I doubt we've activated any magical ward." There was still magic resonating along these walls, perhaps some kind of ward that was permanent? He closed his eyes, imagining Master Viridian and Mistress Cavares sneaking down to the dark part of the archives. He pictured Master Viridian illuminating the way with Light Magic, and coming here, to this very spot, and having the way magically open for him. That was it. Light Magic.

He stepped back and cast a spell summoning a small amount of Light Magic. With the golden light burning knife-edge shadows across the stone wall, Talis heard a rumbling sound as the end of the stone corridor opened before them. Mara beamed and flung her arms around him. They did it, the spell had worked.

Talis stepped down into the dark chamber, allowing the orb of light to illuminate the massive room. The door scraped closed behind them. The ceiling was made of stone blocks held up by enormous pillars, but parts of the walls were exposed earth mottled with rocks and crystals. The center area contained hundreds of wooden cabinets stacked atop broad stone tables. A thick layer of dirt and dust covered the surfaces, as if no one had ever cleaned in the last hundred years.

"We've found it...the Dark Archives." Palarian sauntered over to a cabinet, and ran a finger across the thick dust. "Unused, perhaps? Kept and stored, but not taught or practiced. I wonder if any of the masters have even learned Shadow Magic?"

"I think at least one. I suspect Mistress Cavares has spent time down here learning a few of the spells. At least what she taught me seemed infused with dark magic."

"But wouldn't she have been required to come with Master Viridian?" Mara said.

Talis scratched the back of his head. "Not necessarily. Either she also knows Light Magic, or she set a different opening ward on the door to allow entry using another spell or possibly a spoken password."

"It's likely that she came on her own," Nikulo said. "Master Viridian hated dark magic, I doubt he would have allowed any wizard of the Order to study it unless there was a pressing reason to do so."

"Like an invasion from the Jiserian Empire? Whose sorcerers have mastered Shadow Magic?"

"They're just as bad." Palarian searched for a way to open a cabinet. "They practice dark arts but fail to master the light. They go mad as well. The Jiserians exploit that madness to their advantage. Driving them to even more ruthless acts of war. No sane person could ever be compelled to do that."

"Can't open it?" Mara said, and inspected the cabinet the old man was trying to open.

"Doesn't seem to want to let me open it." Palarian stepped back and thrust his hands on his hips.

"More locked doors down here," Nikulo said, and poked his head around a stone block. "I've found six other stairwells."

"So this is the main chamber?" Talis glanced around the huge, shadow-infested room.

Mara shrugged. "Let's explore. We can always come back later."

"Keep together, you never know what's lurking down there." Talis pictured the shadow creatures from the Underworld.

"You're telling me the archives have some kind of shadow guards?" Mara said.

"Who knows what your Order placed down here." Palarian sniffed the air like he caught a hint of some secret. "Could be magical wards with all manner of spells behind them, or perhaps the young master is correct, there might be shadow creatures farther down, guarding their secrets."

Talis furrowed his brow as he ran a hand along a cabinet. "Or the Dark Archives themselves, the scrolls and tablets and runes, they might be so infused with Shadow Magic that the creatures are compelled to be near them."

"I've caught a hint of something important down this corridor." The sorcerer stalked towards one of the stairwells off to the far corner of the chamber. "Be on guard."

As Talis followed Palarian, stepping quietly, Mara flanked along his left side. Her face held the expression of pure terror and her arms trembled. The room seemed to darken as they approached the stairwell. They took several steps down, and a wind gusted up, smelling of rotten corpses and sulfur. The same smell as the Underworld.

Mara gripped his arm, and glanced up at him like she didn't want to take a step further. Palarian had entered a large, misty room with a massive, swirling shadow portal lying flat in the center of the floor. Lightning charges struck the air above the portal. There were four white crystals on each cardinal corner. This was a World's Portal, similar to the one created by Aurellia at the Temple of the Sun.

"Ah…here it is. The one spoken about hundreds of years past."

"What is this portal?" Talis gaped inside, catching glimpses of other worlds and other places within those worlds.

"This is known as the Portal to Many Worlds." Palarian fingered a stone altar in front of the portal. "If you have the appropriate runes, the portal will take you to your destination of choice. The runes are placed here, in these slots. Unfortunately for many wizards in the past, who've placed incorrect runes, the portal only led them to their deaths."

"And right now death is stalking you," Mistress Cavaress said, stepping out from the shadows.

Talis spun around and raised his hands defensively.
How did she know they were here?

11

The Mistress Disapproves

"Relax, young apprentice, I mean you no harm. This one, however..." She inspected Palarian up and down, an expression of disgust and curiosity on her face. "How did you ever convince these children to grant you access to the Temple archives?"

The sorcerer spread his arms wide in a gesture of supplication. "The young master must have balance in his instruction—"

"Yes, yes, or he'll go mad. Do you take me for a fool? Why do you think I've been teaching him Shadow Magic?"

"You have?" Talis said, and stared at Mistress Cavares.

"Runes are often disguised for teaching the dark arts, and of course the other wizards avoid Rune Magic. Our little outing in the swamplands? Dark magic combined with summoning the shadow gods."

"But why did you do that? Ralakh Lei was killed because of the ward we cast, and now Naru is at war...."

"Was that truly the reason?" Mistress Cavares puckered out her lower lip and placed a hand on her chin. "I think not... Ralakh Lei tempted fate many times and the gods called their just due...his life. Internal strife amongst the Royal Houses has been brewing for months now."

"And Master Viridian?"

"He refused to acknowledge the dark gods he secretly worshipped. And they struck him down for it...and many others in the Order like him. Fear not, child, you're not at risk. At least not by the gods." Mistress Cavares glared at Palarian.

"I mean the boy no harm." The sorcerer bowed low, a look of mock humility on his face.

"Then why have you led them here?" She aimed her gaze at the rune slots in front of the portal. "Planning to go somewhere? All who have tried in the past have failed, and by failure I mean their total disintegration."

"Ah, but they lacked my extensive knowledge of runes." Palarian flashed a hideous grin. "I daresay vaster than your meager knowledge."

"You claim superior knowledge? Prove it."

The sorcerer flourished four rune tablets and placed them in the rune slots. Without hesitation, he leapt inside the shadow portal and disappeared.

"Has he just killed himself?" Mara studied the portal for signs of movement.

"Oh, we can only hope that's the case." Mistress Cavares rolled her eyes, and glanced around the room.

Moments later, a shimmering silver portal appeared on the side of the room, and Palarian stepped through, his eyes beaming.

"Did you miss me? As you can tell, the portal failed to disintegrate me. Why do you suppose that is the case?"

"Do enlighten us…" Mistress Cavares sighed icily.

"Those four runes returned me to my study amongst the snowy pines of the Island of Tarasen. Of course since I've now been to the archives, it was simple for me to return using a portal."

"I thought you said you don't know Shadow Magic?" Mara said.

"That wasn't Shadow Magic…portals can come in different colors, so to speak."

"So I take it you were responsible for teaching them the portal spell?" Mistress Cavares frowned at Palarian.

The sorcerer waved a hand dismissively. "They already possessed that knowledge, and a shadow portal spell at that."

Mistress Cavares raised an eyebrow at Talis. "This day has been strange, indeed. Tell me, stranger, why are you in need of a World's Portal? You have the smell of the ancients on you."

"I long for home." Palarian sighed. "Alas, I tire of your world, it's time for me to return, if I can."

"Well, I'm afraid to disappoint you. After the war with the Jiserians, their summoned demon destroyed the crystal underneath the temple. Luckily these archives were not damaged, however the power source for the portal was lost. There's enough residual energy in these small crystals to allow porting within our world, but not nearly enough for whatever purposes you desire. Does this come as a surprise to you?"

"Indeed, yet not totally unexpected." Palarian glanced at Talis. "However, doesn't this one hold the power of the black crystal within his grasp?"

"Why should he help you? And furthermore, I'm sure he lacks the knowledge of casting World's Portals. None of the Order possess such knowledge. And I doubt you know of it, either."

The sorcerer spread his arms wide in an expression of defeat. "Such a shame, really. I was hoping this would be easier. That my story would bring pity on an old man, trapped on an alien world. But it appears I am wrong."

Mara gazed at him sadly, and stepped close. "Isn't there another way back home?"

Palarian looked up, holding back tears above a wicked smile. "Yes…I'm sure there is. You've given me an idea, dear." From within his robes he tossed something at Mara that looked like a giant moth. The moth's wings, black and grey and copper, expanded to a size larger than a man, and enveloped Mara in several flutters. The sickening pattern of the wing wrapped itself around her body, creating a sticky translucent cocoon.

Though shocked, Talis aimed his hands at the sorcerer and shot out quick bursts of Light Magic.

The sorcerer cried out in a shrill, hideous wail, and raised his fingers to the sky while falling down on his knees. "Stop…stop, you'll kill her!"

Talis ceased his casting after he noticed the cocoon around Mara had darkened and dried, a crust forming around the latticed edges. Mara's eyes went wide in terror and her hands were clutched to her throat as if she'd couldn't breathe.

"Don't you want her to live, boy?" Palarian pushed himself slowly up to his feet. "The cocoon is wounded because of your spell. Don't you want to nurture her lungs with air?"

"Yes, yes! Anything, please." Talis fell to his knees in front of the sorcerer, waves of terror and confusion rolling through his mind.

The old man's wrinkled mouth curled into a snarl. He hurled a ball of silver light from within his sleeve and the cocoon returned to its bright, clear state. Mara gasped, able to breathe now, but she still fought against the cocoon, kicking and punching at the thick shell.

Talis raised a hand to the cocoon, and placed it near where Mara's hand was. He mouthed the words *be calm* to her, and she nodded and lifted her hand over his.

"Now, that's better, don't you think? You all seem in a much more cooperative mood. Perhaps you'll listen to an old man's wishes?" Palarian's yellow-gold eyes glinted with purpose as he studied them.

"Leave the girl out of this," Mistress Cavares said, striding forward. "If you need anyone as a hostage, take me instead."

"Oh, now really…" The sorcerer puckered up his lips. "I doubt the boy would care all that much about your old pathetic life. Would he? But this young tender one, so very close to his heart. And to the fat one as well." He glanced at Nikulo.

"Why don't we all get comfortable." Palarian snapped his fingers and four ornate chairs appeared around the cocoon. He motioned them to sit.

"So I've deduced several things. First, these young wizards learned an extremely rare portal spell on their own, which is highly unlikely. Secondly, their experience took them to Lorello and to Darkov, that ancient city formerly ruled by a sorcerer named Aurellia. Since from the stories I've heard it sounds as if Aurellia has left this world, am I correct?"

Talis suspected his account told to the Order of the Dawn had been leaked to Palarian's spies. And perhaps Palarian had access to Darkov as well, or maybe he once lived there with the other ancients. Talis caught a glimpse of Mara's frightened eyes and vowed to do anything to help her.

"Good. Then my final deduction is that some piece of knowledge passed from Aurellia to these young masters…allowing them to gain knowledge of the shadow portal spell. Am I also correct on this account?"

Nikulo sunk his head, and the sorcerer took this as an indication of guilt. "Ah, this one knows something of such knowledge. You're willing to cooperate, are you not?"

"I'd rather cram a dagger down your throat." Nikulo glared at Palarian. "But since I find myself at your mercy, yes, I'll participate in your little game. I did acquire a scroll from Aurellia's library. The Tandria Scroll."

"No!" Mistress Cavares gasped. "Tell me you didn't touch it! How could you have been so foolish? Don't you realize the scroll is poisoned?"

Nikulo frowned, his face twisted in an expression of confusion. "Poisoned? But I've not been affected...."

"But you have." Mistress Cavares stood and strode over to Nikulo. She shifted his head to face the light from the portal. "Your eyes, tinged grey at the edges. Will thicken over time...get worse. You have maybe a month to live, I'm afraid."

Nikulo paled and recoiled from her. He opened his mouth as if to speak, but closed it instead.

"But we touched the scroll as well!" Mara said.

Mistress Cavares shook her head. "A magical ward with a poison spell was cast on the scroll. Only the first person to touch the scroll would be affected. I'm sorry..."

"How do you know all this?" Talis stared in amazement at Mistress Cavares.

"Aurellia is an infamous runemaster. He sets wards on many objects, doors, entrances, even people. I've heard a story about another scroll killing a famous wizard of the Order. The symptoms were the same."

Palarian chuckled. "Dabble in Poison Magic and get poisoned yourself. How clever. Sounds to me that if the fat one is to be cured, he must seek out Aurellia. Perhaps the sorcerer intended it that way? Do you have something he desires?"

The black crystal. Or did Aurellia want Talis himself to train and twist and warp as his apprentice?

"No matter. Do you possess this Tandria Scroll now?" The sorcerer gazed curiously at Nikulo.

As Nikulo unraveled the scroll, Palarian plucked it from his hands. "Ah, yes…let me read here a moment… Yes, the master scroll to many Poison Magic secrets. And buried here within, the knowledge of several rare portal spells. As I suspected!" He tapped his finger on the scroll. "The World's Portal spell. Indeed, Aurellia wanted you to find this spell. Without a doubt, he expects you will come to the world he's escaped to."

"Then it appears we have no choice." Talis eyed Mara's terrified expression. "What do we have to do?"

The sorcerer's mouth opened in a gleeful expression of victory. "This scroll alone is not enough to cast a World's Portal. There are many bindings to cast first. Bindings of Shadow Magic." He glanced at Mistress Cavares. "I believe the archives possess this knowledge?"

"This is unknown to me, I haven't mastered portals. I would venture to say Talis is the first of our Order to gain this knowledge."

"How typically stupid of your *Order*. You possess scrolls of ancient knowledge and yet you fail to put them to good use?" Palarian scoffed in disgust. "I suppose we have no choice but to search your archives. I know the names of the bindings in the ancient language. Do you at least have a key or a method to open the archive cabinets?"

Mistress Cavares narrowed her eyes at the sorcerer. "Do I look like an utter fool?"

"Now, now, I was raised to have better manners than that. A simple yes will suffice. Good. Shall we search?"

As Palarian turned to head up the stairs, the loud clapping of boots against stone could be heard in the chamber upstairs. Talis tensed, was it the guards of House Lei come to arrest him? He fingered a rune in his pocket containing a portal spell to the temple. He would cast it in a moment if he needed to escape with Mara. Perhaps there was a way for him to remove the shell she was encased in.

"Talis!" shouted his father, Garen Storm. He was flanked by his captain of the guard and Master Grimelore. After he paused to catch his breath, Father grasped Talis's arm. "They've gone to destroy the Temple…House Lei and many of the Order, and all their guardsmen."

Without hesitation, Talis placed the rune and cast the binding near Mara.

"I'll stay here and search the archives," Palarian said. "For the sake of the girl's life, do not attempt to damage or open the cocoon. Only my magic can remove it without killing her."

Talis scowled at the sorcerer, then stepped on the ground where the ward had been placed, and Nikulo helped him tug Mara's cocoon through the portal. Thunder rumbled from inside.

12

Under the Temple

Talis could hear the patter of hail and the booming of thunder strike the temple roof. Why were his own people trying to destroy the only thing that could save them? Lightning flashed outside, striking the beams and rafters, sending a shower of dust and smoke over their heads. Nikulo covered his mouth and coughed, and motioned Talis outside.

"She'll be safe in here," Nikulo shouted.

Talis studied the heavy wooden beams above, then nodded, and followed him outside. Charna yowled when she saw Talis approach.

"Go inside with Mara, keep her safe." Charna padded inside the temple.

Talis rushed around a corner and ran headlong into a Lei guardsman wielding a broadsword. Talis dodged the man's quick thrust, and shot a burst of focused wind at the soldier's chest, catapulting him a hundred feet back into the arms of several wizards casting spells outside.

A band of guardsmen fell to their knees and raised their shields defensively.

"I don't want to hurt you," yelled Talis. "Just leave the temple and go home!"

Archers from the rear flanks sent a barrage of arrows at Talis and Nikulo's position. Talis inhaled the breath of fire and cascaded a wave of flame into the sky, incinerating the assault. The guardsmen wielding shields had edged up during his casting, and were now dangerously close. Talis shot another windstorm at the men, but their shields deflected most of the power until they could bear no more and the force of the wind yanked them upwards and back over fifty feet down the hill.

"Watch out!" Nikulo shoved Talis aside as a lightning bolt struck the ground near where Talis had stood. The bolt singed Nikulo's leg and he cried out in pain.

Talis glanced around. There were wizards positioned everywhere, most cast spells directly at the temple, and only a few targeted Talis and Nikulo. Talis didn't want to kill his own people, but he couldn't have them destroying the temple either. Smoke billowed out from the rafters above.

"We have to retreat…under the temple."

Nikulo nodded, his eyes filled with despair. Why had it come to this? Mara's own father ordering this destruction? If he only knew his daughter was here. They ducked inside the burning temple and darted around to where Mara lay trapped, her eyes screaming as she glanced up at the beams aflame.

Talis motioned Nikulo to grab the other side of the cocoon, and they hauled Mara deeper into the temple, where a stone stairwell descended underneath. Charna darted down the stairs in front of them.

In the forming of the temple complex, Talis had ordered something different: twenty-two layers of five-feet wide stone blocks, and a stairwell that wound down and around until reaching the secured chamber housing the black crystal.

There was only one way in and out. And no guardsmen or wizard could enter without facing the power of the black crystal.

"Now we wait." Talis mouthed the words *it's okay* to Mara, and placed a hand on the cocoon. She smiled and responded back, her eyes calmer now.

Nikulo limped over to the side, and sat on a stone block. He withdrew a vial from his backpack, and dumped the contents onto the burn on his leg. He winced, and placed a hand over the wound. The area around his leg glowed golden for a moment, and his face relaxed as if the healing had worked.

"Better?" Talis said, and Nikulo nodded feebly.

After awhile the smoke wafting down the stairwell intensified, and Talis occasionally sent bursts of wind up the stone hole, pulling in fresh air from vents built into the sides of the stone room. They allowed air inside the deep chamber, but were small enough to bar entrance.

"We're vulnerable down here...I don't like it." Nikulo sniffed, glancing around the enormous chamber. The black

crystal seemed agitated, and pulsed with fine lines of
iridescent light.

"This gains us some time at least. We'd be dead trying
to fight above."

"Unless you killed them all first."

Talis frowned. "Are you serious? I can't do that to my
own people. They're just deluded."

"And intent on killing you and razing the temple.
That's enough cause for me to fight back…for the good of
Naru." Nikulo glanced over at Talis, then exhaled a heavy
sigh. "Why do we even bother helping a people that
obviously cares little about being helped?"

"My family and yours care. Mara cares." Talis smiled
at her. "It's just her family."

"It's all a plot by House Lei. The king is dying, the
healers fail to treat him properly, and Viceroy Lei will try to
take over Naru. The common people will lose."

Talis stood suddenly, realizing it was quiet upstairs.
Had they stopped?

Then the fresh smell of rain and wet smoke came
wafting down the stairwell.

"Perhaps the others of the Order have stopped them?"
he said, and peered up into the stone stairwell. Or had
father sent his troops to rescue them?

A trickle of grey water crept down the stairs. Why was it
raining over the temple? Sun always fell over the temple,
despite any storm that assaulted Naru. The trickled
bubbled up to a gush of smoke and ash-tainted water,

spreading over the stone floor. Then it came to him at once. The wizards were casting Water Magic, summoning storm clouds over the temple.

They were trying to drown them.

Soon the water turned to a flood and the floor was covered in water up to their ankles.

"Any ideas?" Nikulo said, stepping up onto a stone block.

"I do, actually." Talis chuckled. "A truly hideous idea."

He retrieved a rune from within his vest, and placed it on the ground in front of the stairwell. As he closed his eyes, he pictured Viceroy Lei's office, cast a binding spell, and stepped on the magical ward. A shadow portal appeared, and the water slowly poured inside.

"Where does that go?"

"I've been very bad… I fear Mara's father won't be pleased at all."

The water kept gushing stronger until it poured a river down the stairwell. But the portal kept funneling it all away.

"That's enough water to flood a city. How long can you keep the portal open?"

"Longer than all those wizards of the Order can keep it up. They have no crystal to power their magic. I do. Viceroy Lei is going to be so angry when he hears his office and first floor is flooded."

"You didn't!" Nikulo grinned, and glanced up the stairwell. "He's going to jump like he's shat fire!"

"I'd pay gold to see that." Talis glanced over at Mara. "I hope she can't hear us."

Mara raised her hands as if to say, What's going on?

"Better to let her hear about it later, I think." Nikulo waved to Mara.

The water slowed back to a trickle, and Talis could hear shouts echo down the stairs. Some unlucky guardsman had probably been ordered to scout the damage. Boots clapped tepidly against stone. Talis and Nikulo dragged Mara's cocoon off to the corner, away from the line of sight.

"Let them think we've gone through the portal," Talis whispered.

"Then what do we do when they come down in force?" Nikulo frowned.

"I'll think of something."

Nikulo shook his head and muttered something that sounded like *pig's arse*. Talis gave Nikulo a two-fingered marching man's salute (also known in some parts as beggar's rear gushing revenge). Nikulo displayed his tongue and made an obscene gesture. Talis was about to up the insult ante when he caught sight of Mara's disgusted face. She pointed behind them.

A quad of elite guardsmen with banded leather across broad bare-chests marched around the shadow portal. One spotted Talis, and whistled for the others to flank around. Talis grinned and motioned them closer. He was feeling feisty.

"We're not here to kill you, young master." The first guardsman hefted a dual-bladed great axe, and twirled it around like he was anxious to use it.

"Well then put your weapons down and find some ale at a tavern to nurse your problems." Nikulo fingered his temple, and the guardsman's face struggled for a moment. His eyes flipped around in his sockets and he spun around and tackled two of his allies, and they all went tumbling inside the shadow portal. The remaining guardsman fled up the stairs.

"Do you think they're getting tired yet?" Talis contorted his lips in a gesture of doubt.

"The wizards are certainly spent. And I imagine after seeing that last guardsman flee like a donkey's fart, the rest will find their paltry egos crushed." Nikulo bared his teeth and clapped arms with Talis.

After waiting almost half an hour, Talis gestured Nikulo towards the stairwell. Nikulo nodded, and they stalking upstairs. Talis paused and listened. Everything was quiet above. Charna dashed out ahead of them, and they chased after her.

The temple was a wreck of charred and smoking beams. The image of the destroyed old Temple of the Sun flashed in his mind's eye. Talis felt a knot ball up in his stomach. How could his own people do this? Disrespect the Goddess Nacrea in a way so hideous and appalling. He frowned as he scanned around the temple complex, spying the once beautiful fountain now kicked over. The water from the spring spilled around the broken base.

"At least they've left." Nikulo shielded his eyes from the setting sun. The day was worn and tired, as if all the energy of the city had been expended on the assault of the temple.

Talis spied a swirling smoke trail rise from the upper part of Naru. Most likely his father's guardsman were fighting with House Lei. More bloodshed. He sighed and wished it would all just end. In many ways he blamed himself for casting the binding spell on the ward in the swamplands. None of the fighting would have happened if Ralakh Lei were still alive.

A silver portal appeared, interrupting his thoughts. Palarian strode through, eyes shining with pride. In his arms he clutched several ancient-looking scrolls. But his face quickly darkened as he surmised the situation.

"Did you protect the crystal?"

Talis nodded somberly, and narrowed his eyes at the sorcerer. After all that had happened, all he could think about was the crystal and its power? Talis wanted to murder him. He told himself he would after the sorcerer freed Mara. If he could get to him.

"Teach me your spell, old man, and I'll summon your way home. You'll let Mara go free?"

"I'm afraid it's not that easy." Palarian squinted at Talis as if trying to look through him. "You have hateful eyes towards me. Don't judge me so harshly, young wizard. I never intended to harm your girl. Desperate times call for desperate maneuvers."

He sniffed the air and his face paled. "I'm afraid we've not much time, I sense something...ill."

"What do you mean not that easy? I'll only help you if you let Mara go."

"No, no... you'll help me regardless. I can't have you obliterating me. Now hurry up, take me to the crystal!"

Talis stared into the sky where the sorcerer had glanced. He blocked the sun and squinted. Was that a dark cloud approaching from the south? His heart dropped, speeding up to double time. Could it be another Jiserian attack, now at the worst possible time?

Palarian yanked Talis's arm and dragged him towards the stairwell.

"But, wait, I think I spotted—"

"I clearly said we have no time! And for you that means you have no more time, if you want to save her. If I die she dies. Now quickly, let's go!"

At the chamber of the black crystal, Talis caught sight of Mara gazing at him questioningly. Charna padded up alongside, and hissed at the old man. The sorcerer unfurled four scrolls and spread them out over a stone block. He tapped a spot, his finger twitching.

"Here is the binding for the south, and over here the north...here's the west binding. This one took me quite awhile, but I finally found the east binding as well. Your

Order's ridiculous archives have no categorization! Can you believe that?"

Palarian spun around, searching the chamber. "Where are the blank runes? We need runes. Do I have to do everything myself?" The old man flourished several runes from within his robe's sleeves, and handed them to Talis. From a newly-formed mist the sorcerer withdrew an gold inscribing tool.

"Yes, only the finest for these bindings. Gold, yes, shadows and gold. Silver would be prudent, but we have no time." The sorcerer pointed out two ancient characters on the scroll. "Scribe!"

An enormous boom sounded above and the gongs of Naru struck, warning of an attack. The Jiserians were here. Talis felt the old man's leathery hands twist his head back to the task of inscribing the rune.

"Focus, focus! We have four more runes to scribe." Talis cleared his mind and completely gave himself to memorizing the rune characters. If he was ever to save Mara, he had to try and recreate the bindings and the World Portal spell. Her life depended on it.

He finished all four directional runes. The sorcerer flashed a quick smile. "Excellent, you've done well. Now the final rune. Fatso! The Tandria Scroll please."

Nikulo scowled at the old man and handed over the scroll.

"These characters are tricky, if you only look once or twice you'll see the wrong character. Stare a third time and the true form will appear. Remember, often scrolls are scribed with magic, with tricks like these." Palarian watched Talis inscribe the final rune. "Good, now cast the bindings. Simply picture south when you bind north, and east when you bind west…you get the idea. Now go! No, place them in their cardinal directions. Yes, that's right."

Outside the droning and booming sang out as if it possessed the whole sky. Talis suppressed the urge to glance up the stairwell, knowing he had to finish the bindings quickly.

When he completed all four directions, he went to place the World's Portal rune, but Palarian clasped his arm. "Wait…this kind of portal requires something special. Since you've never been there before, you need another set of runes to guide the spell."

The sorcerer carefully removed four runes from a leather satchel at his waist. "I've been saving these for a very long time. He kissed each rune with his dried, wrinkled lips, and placed them on the ground.

"Now, position your rune above these four. Blink seven times to glimpse the true characters. That will suffice, now close your eyes and picture those runes, they'll guide your mind to that world, that world far away beyond the stars. Good… Now cast your binding."

Talis did as commanded, and ensured he'd memorized the rune characters for the destination. Palarian stepped on the magical ward, and an enormous World's Portal the height of the chamber appeared.

The sorcerer smiled like a mischievous boy who'd been caught in a lie. "Do not follow through the portal." He flicked a wrist and the cocoon entrapping Mara spun around and flew inside the World's Portal. Talis cried out, and reached to grasp for her, but she was already gone.

"I'll be waiting on the other side." Palarian glowered at Talis. "If I see you come through before the portal closes, I'll let the cocoon eat her up. I swear it."

The old sorcerer turned and leapt inside the World's Portal, and Talis clenched his fist until his arm went numb.

13

An Impossible Choice

A splintering sound echoed through the stone chamber. Talis spun his head around and stared in horror as a massive crack grew along the center of the black crystal. If the crystal shattered, he'd never have a chance to save Mara.

"Close the portal!" shouted Nikulo.

"How?" He'd never actually closed portals before, they just usually did so on their own. Talis could feel a dry, dusty wind smelling of cinnamon and smoke blowing from the other side of the portal.

"I don't know, just try anything before the crystal shatters."

So Talis closed his eyes and pictured the four runes of the portal's destination. He imagined wiping away the runes, and after awhile he felt the wind die down. He opened his eyes and saw that the portal had disappeared.

Talis and Nikulo gaped at the crystal, watching to see if the splintering would continue. After a few seconds it stopped, but the crack had spread over most of the crystal. If they'd waited half a minute longer, they would've been too late.

"She's gone." Talis sunk to the ground, wishing Palarian would've taken him instead of Mara.

"We still have a chance of finding her." Nikulo aimed his chin at the scrolls still sprawled out on the stone slab. He ran a hand along his neck. "And...I don't want to die, Talis."

A series of booms and explosions echoed down the stairwell. The Jiserians were here. Talis and Nikulo raced up the stairs and gazed at the sky filled with inky-black stains: Jiserian sorcerers and necromancers in flight. The invaders remained far away to the south, apparently trying to keep their distance from the now destroyed temple. Was the Jiserian invasion timed with the assault on the temple? Talis frowned, thinking of Viceroy Lei and their ailing king, suspecting a traitorous alliance.

"Let's try something," Talis said. "Go down and watch the black crystal while I attack the Jiserians. Yell if any cracks or splinters expand or if new ones appear."

Nikulo nodded, and darted down the stairwell. After Nikulo yelled he was ready, Talis focused his mind on a group of Jiserians clustered far to the south. He drew in the power of the setting sun and held in the energy until it built up to a unbearable frenzy. Through his palms he released an enormous blast that lit up the sky around the Jiserians in a blinding flash.

"Stop!" Nikulo shouted, his voice echoing up the stone stairwell. "It's splintering!"

Talis inhaled the air of the failing sun, and gazed across the scene of his city under siege. Streams of spiraling black mist rained down from the skies onto city walls and buildings and towers. Lightning and fire and storm shot up from the city in response. Already puffs of smoke from scattered fires throughout Naru rose into the air. Could he really leave his city unprotected now, at the time when they needed him the most?

Then he thought of Mara, entrapped in that hideous cocoon, and the sorcerer... Talis clenched up his fists until he could feel his neck flushed and tensed. He would kill him, murder him for what he'd done to Mara. Taking one last look at Naru, he turned to face the stairwell, and rushed down, having made up his mind. He had to save her, no matter what. And whatever poison Aurellia had infused in the Tandria Scroll, there had to be a cure. Saving Mara was far more important than fighting the Jiserians.

When Talis reached the bottom, Nikulo stood staring at the splinters spidering across the black crystal. "Do you remember all the runes and the sequences?"

"For yours and Mara's sake, I hope so."

"That last attack was too much for the crystal... Did you do enough damage to repel the Jiserians?"

Talis shook his head, remembering the scattered clouds of sorcerers attacking from various positions over the city. "But if it's good news, I believe Viceroy Lei's formed an alliance with the Jiserians."

"I wouldn't doubt that he'd do such a thing. Hard to believe that traitor is Mara's father."

Another splinter area inside the crystal rang out a sick sound like the fracturing of a tree limb.

"We better hurry!" Talis scanned the four scrolls spread out on the stone block, then glanced around quickly, searching, his heart thumping fast.

He realized he had no empty rune tablets.

"I'm so stupid! How could've I left all my empty runes inside the workshop upstairs?" He lifted the gold inscribing tool that Palarian had left.

Nikulo sighed, and tapped the side of his head. "Just open a portal to Mistress Cavares's workshop, and be quick about it! You do have lots of portal runes, right?"

Talis nodded, and bent down to place the rune. He cast the binding spell, pictured Mistress Cavaves's workshop, and without looking at Nikulo, stepped once and entered the portal.

Instead of being dark, flickering shadows danced off the stone walls of her chambers, halos of candlelight scattered throughout the room. Mistress Cavares sat on her old leather chair, gazing into the crackling fire.

"I knew you'd come back. Forget something?" She jerked her head towards the worktable.

"They obliterated the Temple of the Sun. Why would the Order do that?"

Master Grimelore cleared his throat, and joined Master Jai to saunter over to the fireside. Their eyes were kind and fierce as they stared at Talis.

Mistress Cavares exhaled sharply. "The other wizards aren't in the Order anymore. We're all that's left. Those traitors...hungry for power and influence. Willing to sacrifice our king, claiming devilish deeds are justified in the name of seeking peace? Nonsense."

"The Jiserians are above...."

"Let them come! I pity the poor fool who tries to enter these chambers. I fear not our enemies." She glanced at Talis. "Don't worry, they won't destroy our beautiful city. Viceroy Lei has assured us of that...once the king is dead and he's named supreme ruler."

"But where will you go? You can't stay here forever." Talis handed her a portal rune. "Here, take this."

A smiled curled up the corner's of her lips, and she coughed a chuckle. "So kind, boy, you were always kind. If only the others were more like you, we'd live in a different world. Where kindness not cruelty reigned. Will we find this world someday?"

She pushed herself up, and clapped her hands together. "Time is short. You're leaving us, are you not? I see it's true. Well, before you go, I've packed supplies for you, and brought you your father's sword. And Master Grimelore has something for you."

Talis accepted the backpack and his sword, and bowed deeply to Mistress Cavares. "Thank you for remembering me."

Out of the corner of his eye, he caught sight of something inside the fire in the hearth. Talis swore he glimpsed Rikar's tortured face screaming. But when he looked again, there was nothing.

"Is everything all right, young master? Did the flames show you something?" Master Grimelore was somehow now standing next to Talis, his hand on his shoulder. "The flames can be cruel sometimes, take what you see with a good portion of doubt."

Talis glanced up, studying the wrinkles spread across Master Grimelore's forehead. How he had aged so quickly....

"It's all too much...but I know I've got to keep moving on. So much depends on me, I know that now."

"We'll manage here, somehow, don't fret about that." Master Grimelore removed a honed clear crystal from a leather satchel. "You'll need this where you're going. It's simply a shard, found in the Akesian Mountains many years ago, but it will bring you much needed power."

Talis bowed, and received the shard from Master Grimelore. The energy within felt clear and cool and sharp like hundreds of needle pricks on your hand.

"The black crystal has cracked and splintered." Talis studied Master Jai. "The hated crystal will most likely shatter if I successfully cast the World's Portal spell."

"You must find a new crystal, young master." Master Jai strode forward and took Talis's hands. "Our city and your family depend upon that. Without it we are vulnerable."

"I will try."

Mistress Cavares motioned Talis off towards the north. "You must go. Return to us, with your friends safe. And if you can, bring us a new crystal, whatever the gods deem for us, we will accept this time."

Talis bowed, and ran over to the worktable and scooped up several handfuls of empty rune tablets. He glanced one last time at his masters, placed the portal rune and cast the binding.

He caught Nikulo's eyes as soon as he stepped through the portal. A line of sweat dripped down his friend's brow. "I thought you might not make it back."

After Talis spread nine empty runes onto the stone block, he placed four on each cardinal direction, and one in the center, and four below it. He grasped the gold inscribing tool, and began with the first rune for the northern direction. Nikulo helped point out the right location on the first scroll, and then they moved on to the south, the west, and the east. The scrolls only validated what Talis already memorized.

Another hideous crack, louder and booming this time, snapped across the chamber.

"We've got to hurry," Nikulo whispered, wiping the sweat off his forehead.

Talis shook his head. "Doing this right will keep us from being obliterated by a miscast spell."

The World's Portal rune characters were the most archaic of them all, and Talis had selected a larger rune tablet for the spell. At last he carefully inscribed the four destination runes, and sighed, inspecting his work.

"Is it ready?" Nikulo peered over to study the runes. "They look really similar the other runes Palarian had— I can't tell the difference."

"Okay...let's begin." Talis started by casting the bindings for the cardinal directions, remembering to picture opposite directions for each rune.

Enormous cracks and splintering sounded from within the black crystal. Talis was about to glance back, but he kept himself from looking. He raised himself up and stared at the five runes assembled before him. The cardinal runes had turned to blue flame etched on the stone floor.

Talis quickly looked at Nikulo, and after his friend smiled and nodded, took once last look at the four destination runes. He closed his eyes and cast the final bindings, holding a clear image of the archaic characters.

In his mind's eye he saw darkness flashing over a silver-grey sea, undulating across an endless horizon. Clawed hands reached out to grasp Talis, hands to choke, hands to scratch. Then a fire spread across a desolate plain, building up higher and higher until it was a wall covering the sky. The dry, flaky earth crumbled upon itself, and broke away into the blackness underneath.

And the wind poured hard, striking Talis with a force so strong it stretched back the skin on his face and caused his eyes to water. When he opened his eyes he saw the World's Portal open and churning and tearing, like wild dogs ripping flesh.

The black crystal shattered in a brilliant explosion of light and darkness, millions of pieces smashed back by the force of the wind rushing through the portal. Nikulo clenched Talis's arm and yanked him forward, limping, dragging, then crawling inside.

Talis inhaled and stared up at the grey misty sky.

The air smelled like smoke and cinnamon.

14

Chandrix

Charna raised her elegant head and sniffed the warm air, her nose twitching. The lynx's golden eyes, deep and filled with wisdom, gazed at Talis. Then her tail twitched and she turned and leaned forward as if prey lay somewhere out past the bleak rocky landscape.

There were no trees, no grass, no life that Talis could see. The air was thick with smoke, and indeed smelled strangely of cinnamon. Nikulo stood and dusted himself off, bending down and inspecting claw marks on a stone marker with a gold pyramidal cap.

"The portal destination rune characters are here." Nikulo scanned the ground. "Prints…scuffling of boots. See here, these must be the sorcerer's, and here, something dragged…Mara's cocoon? I think we've done it!"

Talis was lost in thought as he squinted staring over the horizon. How long had it been since Mara and the sorcerer had gone through the portal? Perhaps an hour, maybe less. Could they catch up to them?

"Over here, he's freed Mara." Nikulo held up a piece of the now dried and cracked cocoon. "You ready? The tracks lead this way."

Talis didn't feel ready, he felt this foreign world was filled with dark creatures lurking behind the smoky air, but he followed Nikulo anyways as he waddled down the rocky ledge.

"At least it's not cold here... All I brought was my backpack with a few things and the Tandria Scroll."

"I know you don't have any food inside there...and you ate everything back at the temple," Talis said.

"I can't help it I'm always hungry." Nikulo motioned to Talis's backpack. "Anything good to eat in there?"

"Not sure...Mistress Cavares brought me my backpack and gave me this." Talis swung his pack around and displayed the crystal shard. "Should come in handy."

"Crystals don't taste good. What else is in there?"

Talis rummaged around inside the pack, then jumped as he noticed a rock moving on the ground.

"What's that?" He scurried aside and bent down to inspect the rock.

"A shell." Nikulo poked it. "Camouflaged."

"Do we dare turn it over?" Talis shuddered to think what kind of creatures were on this world. So far the bleakness had made him think of the Underworld....

Nikulo flipped the creature over with a rock. The soft pink underbelly undulated with hundreds of disgusting, writhing feet.

"It's like an insect of some kind."

"I wonder if it tastes any good." Nikulo smacked his lips, and snorted. "Spare a little Fire Magic for roasting an ugly bug?"

"If you're really that desperate, then sure why not." Talis scoffed, releasing a slithering flame from his fingertips and let it toast the hideous insect. A high-pitched scream poured out from the creature.

"Noisy little bugger." Nikulo drooled as he watched Talis roast the bug.

Out of the corner of his eye, Talis noticed the ground shifting and swaying. He stopped the flames. Squinting, he spotted hundreds of the same insects crawling towards them.

"Umm…this can't be good."

"What?" Nikulo glanced at Talis.

Talis jabbed a finger at the creatures as he started stepping backwards. "As in we better get out of here fast. I don't think his buddies liked us roasting him."

Nikulo grabbed the roasted bug, and they turned and ran down the hill. "I hope it tastes good, at least."

Talis sent Nikulo a look of disgust. He had to be crazy to even think about eating that thing. After running for ten minutes or so down the flat, sloping rocks, the mist opened up a bit and Talis could see green shrubbery and hints of a forest far off in the distance. He sighed. At least they were on a world with some green and hopefully life other than camouflaged insects.

"Can we take a rest?" Nikulo huffed and coughed and bent over, pressing his hands onto his legs. "I'm not used to all this running."

"You might have at least practiced your sparring in the training arena." Talis sniffed, and grinned at Nikulo. "Just because you lost your partner doesn't mean you have to get out of shape."

"Hey, I was busy…."

Talis chortled at that. "Busy drinking ale and eating roasted pork at the Wretched Farce?"

Nikulo twisted up his nose. "How'd you know I went there?"

"You crack horrible jokes, get far too drunk, and generally make an arse of yourself."

"So you went there as well, then? Hmph. Should've figured so much. You're probably the one brooding in the corner." Nikulo lifted the roasted insect, and scooped out some of the fleshy insides with his dagger. He chewed hesitantly, then his face brightened, and he nodded. "It's not bad at all, a bit chewy, though. You've quite a skill at roasting, not too burnt…and just bloody enough. Exactly how I like it."

Talis dropped his head and shook it from side to side. What was he going to do with him? "That's so disgusting, I can't fathom how you're eating that…thing."

"You've seen me hungry…you don't want me grumpy, right?"

Talis lifted his hands in a gestured of surrender. Then he scanned the ground. The tracks! They'd fled from the horde of insects and forgotten to scan for tracks. Talis slapped his forehead.

"What? Something wrong?" Nikulo tried crunching on the insect's shell and made a sour face. "This part is no good." He spat it out.

"We forgot to follow Mara's tracks!"

Nikulo glanced around, then bent down and farted. Talis backed up, waving away the smell. Gods, he smelled worse than the roasted bug looked!

"You search that way, and I'll look over here," Nikulo said. "We can't be too far off, didn't we run in the direction their tracks led?"

Talis ran his fingers through the sandy soil, and nodded. "But no more than five minutes, and come back. We can't afford to separate."

As Talis trekked off, searching for tracks, he spotted a weird animal scampering between two bushes, like rabbit with an over-sized bottom. Charna crept low and stalked the rabbit, and Talis reached for his bow but realized he didn't have one. He slung around his backpack instead, and opened it.

Inside, the Surineda Map glowed faintly, as if welcoming him. Talis smiled, thinking how kind Mistress Cavares was. Why hadn't he thought of using the map before? As he unfurled the map, he pictured Mara and a golden dot appeared. They were inside a forest. He also pictured Nikulo and himself, and guessed that she was maybe two hours away. They had to hurry.

Talis ran back towards Nikulo, and shouted when he approached him.

Nikulo's eyes brightened. "Did you find her tracks?" He held something behind his back.

"No...but I found this." Talis displayed the Surineda Map.

"It works here on this world? Interesting, let me see...is this Mara?"

"She's pretty far off, maybe a few hours away."

"Well, now that we have this, tracking them will be infinitely easier. Let's go?"

"What's that behind your back?" Talis darted around to get a better view. "Not another one of those insects. If you're hungry, I spotted a fat rabbit down in the bushes."

Nikulo grinned and released the bug. "Rabbits...I could go for some bunny stew."

They bounded down towards the bushes, searching for game. The landscape slowly changed from rocky steppes to grassland with sparse bushes here and there. Talis rested for a moment, and put a hand to his grumbling stomach. Farther out past several clumps of grass rested a small pool of water. When they got closer, Talis could see it was a spring bubbling up, spilling into a brook that meandered down through the grasslands.

Talis kneeled next to the spring, and took a hesitant sip. "It's delicious!"

Nikulo lurched forward and plunged his entire face into the pool. He slurped noisily and shook his wet hair like a dog from a bath. Charna leapt back, surprised by all the flying water.

"Thirsty much?" Talis chuckled at the water dripping down Nikulo's face.

"I've an appetite for life." Nikulo slapped his belly so hard it jiggled. "Speaking of appetite! That's the fattest rabbit I've ever seen!"

He crept towards the animal, and raised three fingers to his temple. The rabbit twitched a bit, then hopped over to where Nikulo had kneeled. "He's a cute bugger. Half of me wants to keep him as a pet, but the larger, hungrier part of me…well, that half always seems to win out in the end, doesn't it."

"How about you keep him until dinner, we've a long ways to go before dark." Talis scanned the horizon, wondering just how late in the day it was here on this world. He withdrew the map and saw that Mara and the sorcerer were farther ahead than before.

"We'd better hurry up."

"I'll carry him." Nikulo stroked the rabbit's velvety brown fur.

Talis shrugged, and trekked along the brook towards a forest filled with limp trees swaying in the breeze. Enormous boulders the size of a house guarded the descent into the woods, and the brook dashed down and around the rocks until slowing in wetlands underneath the trees.

"We might have to go around, unless we want to get wet."

Nikulo pointed at his drenched hair. "Something wrong with wet? It's warm here."

The air smelled stronger of cinnamon here, but the smoke had diminished on their descent. Talis glanced left and right, trying to decide the right way to follow Mara. From what he remembered from the first time he'd checked the map, Palarian had gone directly inside the forest.

"Let's try to find a way inside." Talis leapt from rock to rock, and climbed down the boulder, finding a crevice to make the descent easier. Charna had bounded down the rock face deftly, and was scouting ahead, sniffing something that caught her interest.

Once at the bottom, Talis turned and stared up at Nikulo.

"Well you made that look easy, didn't you?"

"You could always slide down the waterfall." Talis grinned.

To his surprise, Nikulo put the rabbit in his backpack, and found an edge and climbed backwards down the boulder face, discovering notches and crevices to grab ahold of. He pushed off near the bottom, and landed softly.

"I've been practicing." Nikulo wiped his hands and chortled at Talis. "Ever since that embarrassing incident climbing the tree in Seraka, I decided to improve my skills."

"Impressive," Talis said, wondering what else Nikulo had been practicing these last few months.

They found a way inside the thick forest, following a meandering path of moss and ferns that rose above the wetlands. The canopy of menacing trees above swayed gently in the warm wind, casting bladed bursts of sunlight on the lush emerald-green forest floor. The air held the pungent smell of wet rot and herbs like lime and mint and lemongrass, a fragrant explosion in Talis's nostrils.

The path was slow-going, stopping to navigate around swamp-lakes, sink-holes, and clusters of immature trees struggling to rise above the larger canopy. Even more frustrating, whenever Talis scanned the map, it seemed like Mara and the sorcerer were even farther ahead than before they entered the forest.

"Aren't you getting hungry?" Talis said, staring at the rabbit Nikulo held in his arms.

Nikulo came out of his reverie suddenly, and glanced at Talis like he'd just suggested something horrible. "He's quite a nice pet, you know."

"I suppose we could hunt other game. But you can't keep him forever. If you're not careful, Charna's going to have him for a snack." Talis scratched the lynx's chin, and Charna purred noisily.

"Keep that kitty away from my bunny. She can find her own supper out there in the swamp."

As if taking the hint, Charna's tail twitched and she darted off into the bushes.

"It's getting dark." Talis stared above at the mottle of grey and gold-edged canopy trees. As long as they had the Surineda Map, they could track Mara wherever she went.

"Let's go until it's too dark to walk."

Talis followed Nikulo, minding his way around thick ferns and tangle vines that slithered towards him whenever he passed. The forest sprung to life wherever they went. Talis worried about sleeping anywhere in this strange forest for fear of what might come to them in the night. The forest was eerily quiet. Since entering, Talis hadn't spotted a single creature.

Charna returned when the light failed the way, proudly displaying a fat mole wriggling in her mouth. "Well, look what a good hunter you are." Talis smiled at Charna, and received the gift she lay at his feet. "Is this a good enough place to rest for the night?"

Nikulo glanced around suspiciously, petting his rabbit. He shrugged, then sighed in resignation. "Over there, in that stand of trees. Maybe there's more protection from the foliage." He kicked away a tangle vine that was snaking up his leg.

The cluster of young trees had a nest of bark and branches beneath them, with no vines or shrubbery around the base. Talis selected a good stick, and prepared the mole for a roast. He was wary about starting a fire here, in this creepy forest, so he cast careful lines of flame from his fingertips, inhaling the sweet stench of roasted meat.

The rabbit in Nikulo's arms twitched nervously at the Fire Magic, but was calmed by reassuring strokes from Nikulo. At last the roast was complete.

"You're not going to eat all of that, are you?" Nikulo opened his mouth, then wiped a line of drool.

"Aren't you full from eating that mystery meat?"

"Completely unsatisfying. Left me wanting more." Nikulo gazed expectantly at the roast.

"What? More of that hideous looking insect?" Talis shrugged, and took a bite of the roast. "Now this is a feast, a meal worth waiting for."

Nikulo opened his mouth, then closed it, his face forming the expression of a puppy begging. Talis was planning to make him suffer even more, but gave in when his friend allowed a whimper to escape from the back of his throat. He handed him the roast, and snorted.

"What would we do without Charna." Talis dug deep into the lynx's neck fur, relishing the low murmurs and rumblings of appreciation. "I hope you found your supper first, golden-eyed one."

The lynx licked her lips, and bent her head down as if answering. She curled up alongside Talis's legs, and closed her eyes. The night was black as coal now, and the forest had come alive with an explosion of insects chattering and strange animal grunting and hooting noises scattered everywhere.

Talis's eyes drooped heavily as he listened to the sounds, unable to stay awake. Stars flared in his mind's eye, flashes of the sun and ringlets of light. But behind it all hundreds of eyes lumbered towards him in the darkness, calling out to him, singing in a soft, hypnotic rhythm, until he cared little of resisting....

15

Nightmare Forest

Talis jerked awake at the sound of a bird's shriek, and glanced warily around at the dim golden light illuminating the forest floor. Was it morning already? Something smelled rotten, stinking of old mold and fresh vomit. In a panic, he realized that Nikulo was gone. Talis's backpack was stolen, the Surineda Map was missing, and worst of all, the sword that his father had given him, that was gone as well.

What had happened? One moment he'd gone asleep, and the next he'd woken all alone. Now the night was black and cold like the Northlands, and Talis shivered, realizing his cloak was stolen also. He felt like crying, but he was shaking so bad from the cold and the fear of this strange, dark forest, the tears failed to come. Electricity sizzled under his skin, filling his entire body with the feeling that he might die tonight.

He was vividly awake, listening to the birds chirp and complain, the wind scattering leaves across the forest floor, and the moaning and croaking of tree branches above. But one sound stabbed out at his ears, so that all the other sounds faded away, like when you hear a predator stalking you in the night. For it was a predator, and many of them, slithering through the dry leaves, a cacophony of shooshing like a mother putting her baby to sleep.

Yellow, slitted eyes glowed in the dark, moving towards him. Talis rummaged around the ground and found a stick, thick with long, twisted branches. He slashed out at those hideous eyes and writhing shapes, only to find his weapon had dissolved into hundreds of crawling shapes, like black ink spilling from his hands.

A shiver of revulsion ran through him. He sprinted, kicking and clearing a path, knowing there were too many, far too many for him to fight. Past the clustered trees, through wetlands and stumbling over logs and grassy tufts, Talis could hear the sound of the snakes slowly fade into the background. The night was still once more. Sweat drenched his back, and yet his fingers and face were still numb from the cold.

The smell of clear, fragrant water bubbling through the forest instilled the feeling of peace within his mind. He still worried of finding Nikulo and their gear, but the strength of his thirst was greater than that. A moonbeam sliced it's way through the mottled sky and wavering trees, illuminating the stream's mossy edges in white and grey tones.

He kneeled and scooped up two handfuls of black water, then cried out as several rats leapt from his hands. Those tiny feet terrorizing his palms, so close to his thirsty and parched lips. He wanted to scream and scratch and wipe his hands until the rat-stench came off. But he stopped and thought.

This was all a nightmare.

Talis stared at the inky water rippling angrily, and felt a buzzing sensation pulse along the back of his neck. He raised his head and found himself staring out over a vast desert horizon, early morning purple hues tainting the sky. A dragon flew towards him, black shiny scales twinkling in the light of the moon and stars, and its terrible jaws poured forth an avalanche of fire that seared the dry ground, scorching the land. Gold eyes terrorized his soul as the dragon bore down on him. He raised his hands to combat flame with fire but found his powers gone, he was helpless to the onslaught of flame.

The heat kissed his skin, and he smelled the sick stench of burning hair as flames lapped over him. Dying, he refused to feel pain, and instead the bliss of clarity filled his mind. This was just a dream, he told himself, and repeated the words over and over again, until he woke and felt sweat drenching his body.

Nikulo writhed on the ground next to him, moaning and groaning in a fitful dream. Sweat poured from his brow, and he was shivering as the chills possessed his body. Talis shook him and yelled for him to wake up, but his friend was gripped by a far greater force.

A rustling in the trees above caused Talis to glance up and realize they were prey for some creatures descending towards them. He pushed Nikulo up to a sitting position, and slapped him hard on the cheek several times until his friend winced and blinked and opened his eyes.

"Can you stop hitting me?" Nikulo put a hand to his face and rubbed it, staring warily at Talis.

"You were having a nightmare!"

Terror poured into Nikulo's eyes, and after a moment he drooped off to sleep again. Talis felt a sudden wave of sleepiness possess him as well, but fought the urge to close his eyes once he saw Nikulo's reaction.

"Wake up!" shouted Talis, shaking Nikulo again. When the urge to sleep again came strong to him, he realized that the creatures coming towards them were causing the nightmares. They had to escape. But as he dragged Nikulo away, Talis's eyes turned heavy as lead and his legs crumbled in fatigue. He simply couldn't take another step.

The lower branches shook with the weight of the creatures, and flung up as they landed on the ground and made a withering hiss. Hundreds of piercing pale-green eyes bounced in the darkness as the things shambled towards them.

Talis knew they wanted to eat them, to drink their blood and consume their flesh, he could feel malicious cravings flowing from their eyes. He had to fight them, to stay alive and help Mara. She was out there waiting for them to come. He raised his hands and prepared to cast Light Magic and banish the black night.

But just as he tried to cast the spell, a numbing dizziness washed over him, sending him toppling to the ground. He couldn't move and by sheer will alone he kept his eyes open, despite the overwhelming urge to sleep.

Charna darted past him, and Talis swore her fur glowed golden, illuminating the darkness as she bounded after the creatures. He could hear Charna hissing and yowling and the creatures yelping and grunting. Out of the corner of his eye he spied the mottled pink and grey hairless creatures swarm over Charna, dampening her light, casting ugly squirming shadows up to the trees.

Talis found himself roused after the creatures had focused their energies on Charna. He pushed himself up and stumbled towards the creatures. For fear of hurting Charna, he concentrated Fire Magic on the insides of each creature, each spell causing an explosion of blood and organs and hairless skin to shower across the forest. He ducked, trying to escape the sick fragments from splattering onto him.

Soon he finished the last creature, and rushed up to where Charna lay on the ground. Her body twitched. Hundreds of small slashes and teeth marks marred her once beautiful coat. Sadness flooded inside, and he found his face scrunched up as he choked back the tears. She was still alive, and panted weakly, puffs of her breath wafting out into the cold night.

Talis lifted her, and carried the lynx back to Nikulo and lay her at his feet. Talis shook him awake. "You have to help her, Charna is hurt!"

Nikulo's sleep-weary eyes darted open at his words, and Nikulo rummaged around in his pack, withdrawing several vials. He kneeled next to Charna, and quickly poured the vial's contents over the wounds. Charna whimpered and yowled softly, but Talis was pleased to see that she was responding to the medicine.

"What happened to her?" Nikulo laid his hands over her wounds, and light glowed underneath her skin.

"She saved us, but there were too many...."

Nikulo raised an eyebrow, his face curious and dismayed. "Saved us from what?"

"We better get out of here, in case there's more." Talis glanced above at the limbs swaying in the soft breeze. They wouldn't be able to survive another attack, not with Charna injured.

Talis withdrew the Surineda Map from his pack, and spotted Mara far ahead in what looked like a field or a clearing. He put the map away, and swung his backpack around.

"Let's carry her, she's not that heavy." Nikulo wore his pack, and helped Talis lift Charna. She licked Talis's arm, her golden eyes slits, her body purring appreciatively. She truly was a gift from the Goddess Nacrea; she'd saved their lives. Talis said a silent prayer to the Goddess, thanking her for the gift.

As they strode in the direction of Mara and the sorcerer, Talis told Nikulo the story of the creatures and the nightmares. "I did have horrific dreams," Nikulo said. "I was being attacked by a flock of roasted pheasants and barrels of ale. Very strange."

Talis chuckled, and they rested awhile, swapping turns to hold Charna. After carrying the lynx for several miles, Charna twitched, eyes alert, and pounced from his arms. She licked her shoulder, sniffed the air, and bounded off after something.

"Thanks to your healing, she's feeling better." Talis smiled at Nikulo. "I thought we'd lose her."

"We can't lose our precious cat." Nikulo rubbed his chest and grinned. "How far away is Mara now?"

"Far...farther than before when we went to sleep. So they've been traveling through the night."

"Maybe they found horses...or something to ride."

Talis glanced around the sparse forest, and up ahead spotted fields of grass or wheat swaying under a soft breeze. He had an idea. "I think we've been using the map incorrectly."

"How so?"

"Look." Talis spread the map out, and closed his eyes. He told the map of his desire to see people and dwellings and cities. When he opened his eyes, the map zoomed in closer and displayed several farms and a village nearby.

"That's amazing! I never know it could do that... We could rest at that village, it's quite close," Nikulo said, and glanced at Talis.

"Is there any place to truly rest on this world?" Talis could only think of home, and his mother's cooking, and the crackling fire at the hearth. He was tired already of this strange world.

"Let's go. Maybe we'll find an inn." Nikulo pulled Talis's arm and they strode off towards the field. Soon they reached a river meandering through stands of what looked like willow trees, and eventually reached a village surrounded by tall spiked wooden walls. Torches blazed atop each of the towers. The path of the river split right through the village, and underneath the walls.

At the main village gate, a hulking man wearing sheepskin patrolled outside. He held a gnarled wooden staff. When he spied Talis and Nikulo lumbering close, he whistled, and several wolves with glowing red eyes charged them.

16

Fioran Village

Nikulo placed a hand on his temple as the wolves bared their fangs, rumbling and growling as they stalked closer.

"Don't," Talis whispered, holding Nikulo's wrist. "Let's see what they do first."

"Who's out there lurking in the dark?" shouted the man in sheepskin. He marched over, his movements stiff and jerky, as if his leg had been injured.

"Just two young travelers." Talis spread his hands wide in a gesture of peace. "We seek shelter and food for the night."

"Two foolish travelers out on a night like tonight?" The man peered incredulously at them. "And you came from the Vacran Forest?"

Talis shrugged, and glanced back at the dark mass of the distant forest. "We are strangers to your land, and unfamiliar with the dangers that prowl out in the dark."

"And you were waylaid by strange creatures, were you not?" the man said.

"How did you injure your leg?" Nikulo tilted his head sideways, studying the man.

"My leg? Oh, this old war injury?" The man slapped his leg and grimaced. "It pains me much, but I've learned to live with it, I suppose. Why do you ask?"

Nikulo swung around his backpack. "You see I'm a healer, of sorts. I might be able to aid your suffering."

The man laughed and coughed and slapped his chest. "Oh, really now, I've seen them all and to no avail. Their treatments may help for a time, but it always comes back, especially in the winter when it's cold. But thank you for your kind thoughts."

"No, I can actually help. I've the gift of healing magic."

"Magic?" The man's face paled, and he took several steps back, eying them suspiciously. Talis realized they should be more careful revealing too much, especially here in this strange land. He sent a warning glance to Nikulo.

"What my friend means is that sometimes the gods of healing listen to his prayer of supplication." Talis bowed low to the man.

The man's expression softened, and he cleared his throat. "I see... Well you won't be needing that here in the humble Village of Fioran. We've not much use for *magic* here. You may enter and stay for a night, but I expect we'll be wanting you to leave in the morning. Strangers are allowed to stay at the Dancer's Rest, the inn at the far end of town."

Talis and Nikulo followed the man as he limped towards the gates. Charna dashed up alongside Talis, her eyes narrowed at the wolves. The man raised his wooden staff and rapped hard four times. "Open up, you laggards! We've got two travelers that need lodging at the Dancer's Rest."

The small inside gate creaked open, and two boys peered through. "Travelers? At this late hour?"

"Yes, yes, now one of you escort these gentlemen to the Dancer's Rest." The man scowled at Charna. "And keep your cat out of trouble, best keep her locked up in your room, or we'll throw her into the pens with the wolves."

Talis ignored the man's taunt and scooped Charna into his arms. One of the boys motioned them inside where torches illuminated the cobblestone streets, splashing wavering shadows across the mud and brick walls of the houses crammed together. They were the only ones out, except for rats and stray dogs wandering about. The smell of hops and manure and piss infected the air.

"I'm Tad," said the boy. "Why out so late after dark?"

"We got lost," Talis said.

"I'm surprised you didn't get killed." Tad kicked a stone and sent it skittering after a rat darting down a gully. "The only reason we're safe is cause these walls, they keep the nasty creatures out."

Nikulo wrinkled up his nose and frowned, as if all the nastiness were inside the walls. "Hope this inn of yours smells better than here."

"Oh its not so bad...you get used to it." The boy round a corner and motioned to a dilapidated building at the far

153

end of the street. "There she is, the Dancer's Rest. I'll wake the owner and he'll find you a room."

"Looks more like the pig's rest, if you ask me." Nikulo sidestepped a fresh pile of dog poop.

The boy shrugged. "Pig or a dancer, it's all the same, you'll find rest there. Especially now that the fields are still growing. Come harvest time and the place will be packed."

"Lucky for us," Nikulo muttered.

Tad rapped on the front door of the inn, and they waited quite awhile until Talis could hear shuffling sounds come closer to the door. A beefy man with a surly expression on his face opened the door, staring at Talis and Nikulo with suspicious eyes.

"What's the bother all about, waking me at this ghastly hour? You boy? And who are these two, anyways...I've never seen them before." The innkeeper sniffed. "They smell like the forest...I don't like the forest. Why did you bring them here?"

"Master Gilliam commanded us to take them here." Tad's voice went whiny at the sour face on the innkeeper.

Talis felt around in his pocket, and withdrew his coin purse. "We'll pay you for troubling your sleep, kind sir. A room would be greatly appreciated, and breakfast later in the morning."

The innkeeper scowled at the silver coin Talis displayed. "What's this? Is it silver?"

"A silver coin—"

"A coin? What's that. Silver I know, but coin…?" The innkeeper showed Talis a silver ingot. "You're strangers from a strange land. Where exactly are you from?"

Talis glanced at Nikulo, smirking slightly. "I don't think you've heard of it, our land is very far away past the forest and the badlands."

"Hmmm…I've heard rumors of such a kingdom. There was an old man just here last evening, with a girl about your age, but he purchased mules and left before nightfall. Rather strange fellow."

Talis's heart leapt at the news, the innkeeper was talking about Mara! So they had acquired animals to ride, no wonder they were making faster time. How could they catch up to them? They had to find mules or horses of their own.

"Do you think in the morning you could point us to your stables?" Talis eyed Nikulo. "We'd like to purchase horses of our own."

The innkeeper scoffed. "Come on inside, you're letting the cold in. Horses you won't find, but mules… well, perhaps you'll be lucky since it's not harvest season."

Inside, the inn was shabby and smelled of ale and beer and mulling spices. Coals inside the hearth burned low, giving out smoke and barely any light at all. The innkeeper's candle bounced up and down as he trudged along the narrow hallway, and up stairs that led to the rooms. He showed them to a cramped room with a straw bed covered in a tattered green blanket with oily stains scattered across the surface.

Talis winced and covered his nose at the smell. "You don't have anything else, I suppose?"

"Be thankful I'm letting you stay at all." The innkeeper shut the door behind them.

The next day's breakfast of hot porridge and bacon, eggs and potatoes in a hash was a bright spot in an otherwise bleak night. The innkeeper's daughter was another bit of brightness. Nikulo practically glowed when she brought him his food, and actually displayed a wide smile (though he didn't realize bits of bacon stuck were stuck in between his front teeth) when she came again and poured him some hot mead.

"What a girl," Nikulo said, and took a long drink of the honey mead.

"How can you drink that stuff...they make it too sweet."

Nikulo waved the idea away. "She's the sweet one. I'd drink whatever she's pouring."

"Including cow piss?" Talis chuckled, and ate another bite of the potatoes and eggs.

"You're just jealous she's got eyes for me."

The innkeeper's daughter sauntered towards them, her eyes teasing them like she knew exactly what they were talking about. "More mead, kind sir?"

"You can call me Nikulo… And what's your name?"

"Ophellia." She glanced at Talis. "Your friend seems a bit lost...late night?"

Talis yawned, and nodded. "Indeed, and a rather lumpy bed of straw."

Ophellia opened her mouth wide, and glared at her father in the far corner. "I can't believe he stuck you in *that* room. We've plenty better rooms available. I hate him."

"It was that room or out in the forest." Nikulo rubbed his head, his expression displeased at the thought. "That terrible forest, we could have been killed if it wasn't for Charna."

"Charna?" Ophellia said.

"My lynx. She woke us from the nightmares the creatures were causing, and we...escaped. What happened there..." Talis noticed a faded bruise on Ophellia's left eye and stared a little too long until she raised a hand to cover it.

Ophellia leaned in, and whispered, "He beats me, you know. That's why I hate him. I never did him no harm, why does he hit on me so much?"

Nikulo glowered at the innkeeper, and clenched his spoon like it was a knife. Talis studied the girl, sensing sadness and shame. He opened his mouth to say something, but she raised a hand to stop him.

"I better go or he'll suspect something." Ophellia rushed off, pouring mead to the patrons at the other tables.

Talis held Nikulo back as he was about to go after the innkeeper. "Save it for later, I have an idea."

They finished their breakfast, and Talis carried scraps of roasted chicken for Charna. She purred gratefully as he gave her the food. Nikulo took another drink of mead from the mug he'd snuck to the room.

"I wonder if lynxes like mead?" Nikulo said, and tilted the mug towards Charna. She sniffed it, and her eyes brightened. "I guess she does... Whoa, don't go drinking it all, now."

Talis chuckled, and sat back on the lumpy bed watching her eat. He unraveled the Surineda Map and summoned the image of Mara. He frowned.

"They've stopped moving, strange."

Nikulo peered over the map. "Maybe they're resting? They can't keep traveling like that. I wonder where they're going?"

"I wish I knew. Let's pack up and go."

"What's your idea for the innkeeper? I can't stand the idea of that beady-eyed monster hitting on Ophellia."

Talis slung his backpack around, and grinned at Nikulo. "I'll show you."

They found the innkeeper downstairs in a room behind the bar. He was counting silver and copper ingots when he looked up and scowled as they came inside and shut the door behind them.

"What do you two want? You had your breakfast, now get out here."

"There's the small matter of pointing us in the direction of the stables. Our mules?" Talis sauntered over and sat on the man's desk.

"Get off my desk and get out of my inn!" The innkeeper's face went red.

"Are you right or left handed?" Talis said innocently.

"What? What kind of an idiotic question is that?"

"You heard me. When you beat your daughter do you use your right hand or your left hand?"

The innkeeper sprang to his feet, and raised a clenched right fist at Talis. "I'll kill you…."

Talis sent a painful amount of Fire Magic inside the man's right hand, and smiled grimly as the innkeeper cried out and stared in disbelief at his hand.

"What devilry?" The innkeeper flapped his hand, glancing around the room. He sunk his hand into a mug filled with liquid, but it did no good.

"I can make it stop…if you sit down and listen quietly." Talis leaned in and glared at the innkeeper. "Or I can make it much, much worse…."

The man obeyed, terror blazing in his eyes as he stared at Talis.

"Now listen to me very carefully, I've placed a spell on your hand, the hand you've used so shamefully to beat on your own daughter. Are you paying attention?"

The man nodded, and whimpered and cried as Talis sent more fire into the man's hand.

"From now on you'll never lay a hand on her again, do you hear me? If you do, the spell will flare up again and then the pain will be five times as much as you're experiencing now. Do you want to feel what that's like?"

The innkeeper shook his head vigorously, shame and agony pouring from his eyes.

"Good. Leave the girl alone, and you'll be fine. But if you don't..." Talis hung his head as if contemplating terrible things. He stood and went to the door. "Oh, would you be kind enough to introduce us to the stable master? I hate bargaining with strangers."

"Of course...anything, I'll do anything." The innkeeper rose, trembling and staring warily at Talis, and led them briskly down the now bustling villages streets to the stables.

The innkeeper did indeed bargain well for them. Talis and Nikulo walked out with a fresh mule each. When they mounted the creatures, the innkeeper rushed away, not daring to glance back. Talis thought of the innkeeper's daughter, and felt a warm glow spread across his chest. She wouldn't have to deal with his abuse anymore.

"Why do you suppose Mara and Palarian have stopped moving?" Nikulo said, shifting uncomfortably on the mule.

Talis gazed down the grubby street lined with gawkers, merchants and stalls, and then to the end where the eastern gate led towards where Mara and the sorcerer had gone. An enormous man carrying a butchered ham waddled across the street, causing the mules to stop abruptly.

"I have no idea..." Talis wiped his nose. "Do we need supplies?"

Nikulo slapped his forehead. "Supplies!" He jumped off his mule and led the beast over to a vendor selling dried pork, baked sweet potatoes, and roasted almonds. He handed a silver coin to the lady and she frowned, turning over the coin several times, bit it, and finally seemed satisfied.   Nikulo stuffed the pork, sweet potatoes, and almonds into his backpack, and handed more to Talis. Charna nuzzled Talis's hand, and he gave her a piece of dried meat.

The sun glowed orange in the western horizon after they'd ridden most of the day. Every time Talis had checked the Surineda Map, Mara was still in the same place. For the last few hours, a feeling of dread had spread over him. Something was wrong. Even Charna seemed agitated, her tailed twitched as she scanned across the field.

As if sensing his mood, Nikulo cast Talis a reassuring look. "Maybe they've found a place the sorcerer was looking for, or they're visiting someone?"

"Whatever the reason, we'll reach them by nightfall." Talis was fearful of confronting the sorcerer again. Whatever magic Palarian had cast on Mara, he could do that or some other strange kind of magic he'd accumulated over the many thousands of years of his life.

After another hour of traveling through wheat fields and sparse forests, they found themselves quite close to

161

where Mara was on the map. They ventured away from the wheat and into a clearing surrounded by elm trees. In the center of the clearing, there was a campfire burning low, and a figure sat nearby. In the dying light Talis made out a silvery shimmer, an enormous bubble of sorts covering the figure and the fire.

Fear and hope shot through Talis as he recognized Mara. His heart raced, scanning around for Palarian, searching the the fields, preparing himself for battle.

17

Left Behind

Mara stood abruptly, her eyes flared in fear, and raised a hand to stop Talis's advance. Nikulo froze, and glanced at Talis as if wondering what to do. In their race to catchup with Mara, Talis realized he'd forgotten to track the sorcerer's movements as well.

"She's surrounded by some kind of bubble…a magical shield?" Talis frowned, sliding off his mule, and he walked the perimeter around Mara's camp. She pointed at the ground.

"Be careful, Talis," Nikulo said. "Palarian has probably placed magical wards all around her."

Talis took a step back, and sank to the ground. He withdrew the Surineda Map, summoned the image of the sorcerer, and tracked his position as miles east of here. Why had Palarian left Mara all alone here? He scrunched up his eyes and tried to puzzle it out.

From behind, Talis heard a slithering in the grass and a hiss loud enough to drown out his thoughts. A black shape slashed out at him, and he recoiled back in fear, his heart pounding. Nikulo jumped off the ground as another shiny dark thing undulated through the grass where he'd been sitting. Charna swatted the grass with her paw, and in lightning-quick speed snapped back. A glassy black snake's head raised itself up as if inspecting them, its forked red tongue flicking in and out like it was tasting their smell.

"Get back!" Talis shouted, and edged away from the taller grass. Nikulo flanked around to the right, raising fingers to his temple.

In a quick burst, Talis shot fire from his fingertips, causing the grass to erupt in flames. The mules brayed and bucked, terrorized by the fire. Hundreds of giant black snakes rose up at once, immune to the flames, staring at them. Their mirror-like scales shimmered in the firelight.

Talis and Nikulo retreated from the snakes, watching in horror as the giant creatures grappled the mules, sinking their enormous fangs into their bodies, poisoning them until the mules fell over and exhaled for the last time, their eyes open in shock and fear. As Talis continued backing away from the snakes, he felt a tingling sensation run up and down his spine. He quickly glanced around and realized the magical shield around Mara had fallen as he'd passed through it.

Mara rushed over and flung her arms around him. "I thought I'd never see you again."

"We'll never see anyone again if we don't get out of here," Nikulo said.

Talis faced the snakes again, pictured the sun in its strength, and shot out a burst of Light Magic at the reptiles. He could feel the power of the crystal shard aiding him in his casting. But the light only reflected off the glassy black scales, and the snakes slithered closer.

"Are they immune to magic?" Talis said, staring at the snakes winding through the burning field.

Nikulo pushed his way forward, aiming his fingers at the creatures. "I've been meaning to test this spell out."

A stain of ghostly grey and black fibers shot from his fingertips and erupted across the field, finding purchase inside the snake's bodies. "Fight fire with fire, and poison with poison."

Just as the reptiles were about to overtake them, the snakes twitched, bared their fangs, and struck out against air, earth, branch, grass, flame, and even biting each other. Talis, Nikulo, and Mara stayed far enough away from all the mayhem, as the snakes twisted, sprang out, and contorted wildly.

"What did you do to them?" Mara said.

"The poison spell I learned from the Tandria Scroll."

Mara's brow furrowed as she stared at the snakes writhing in agony. "That's disgusting... But, incredibly effective."

Talis slapped Nikulo on the back. All those months Nikulo had spent studying the Tandria Scroll had paid off.

"So the sorcerer created the bubble to protect you?" Talis said.

"He's not a bad person at all," Mara said. "Ruthless, yes, but not evil. He knew you would cast the portal spell

165

and come after him, but he was fine with that. He just wanted to return home."

"And you told him I had the Surineda Map?"

Mara nodded, her eyes careful to see if Talis would be angry. "Palarian wanted to avoid fighting you, so he had to get far enough away. He figured it would take you some time to create the runes and cast the portal spell."

"But why didn't he leave you at an inn back in the Fioran Village?"

"He said those villagers couldn't be trusted, they often kidnapped strangers and took them as slaves, especially girls." Mara shook her head and exhaled in disgust.

Nikulo wrinkled up his forehead. "So what do we do now? We're out here in a foreign world, and Naru is under siege by the Jiserians."

"And by House Lei."

"What?" Mara stared incredulously at Talis.

So Talis told her the story of what he knew, of the plots and intrigue surrounding the king, and rumored shadowy alliances with the Jiserian Empire. She winced at the story of her father leading an attack against the Temple of the Sun.

"How could he do that?" she shouted, slapping her hands on her thighs. "He promised me he wouldn't hurt you if I stayed away from you."

"You promised him you'd stay away from me?" Talis muttered.

"I didn't mean it, and I made the sign of Trickster with my left hand. He was constantly bothering me about it!"

"That's okay." Talis ran a hand along her back. "Somehow we have to sort out the mess back home, bring things back to normal."

"Normal?" Nikulo scoffed. "Things have forever changed. We've changed. And unless we find a massive power source like the black crystal, we'll be stuck here on this world forever."

They remained quiet for a while, listening to the fire hiss and crackle across the grass field. The air was thick with smoke, and Talis was lost in his thoughts. What would they do? The vision of Rikar trapped in that storm flashed in his mind's eye. Did they have a duty to help him? Then a cold chill spread across his stomach.

The vision and the knowledge of the portal...it was all Aurellia's doing.

Aurellia's words echoed in his mind: *You know so little. But one day you might figure out a thing or two. If you dare, you'll search for me in your dreams. If you're afraid and cower in that city of yours, I'll return and consume everything you hold dear.*

So that was it, Aurellia had sent Rikar to search for Talis in his dreams, and when that wasn't enough, he sent the Jiserians to destroy his city. And all the while Nikulo had been learning the Tandria Scroll. Did Aurellia send Palarian to them as well? What did Aurellia want from them?

"Are you okay?" Mara sat next to him and leaned her head on his shoulder. It felt wonderful to have her close again.

Talis smiled warmly at her. She blushed and nudged him in the ribs.

"At least we're all together again," Mara said. "Why don't we have a look at the map?"

"Everything that's happened seems to have been planned by Aurellia." Talis unfurled the Surineda Map, and felt the warmth slither up his hands from the map's power.

He closed his eyes and pictured Aurellia, and instantly the sorcerer's wrinkled, gaunt face appeared, gazing at him with a why-have-you-waited-so-long look. Talis tried to resist the vision, hated seeing Aurellia's hideous face, but somehow he couldn't break the connection.

"It's been a span of time since I've seen you, young wizard," Aurellia said. "You've ignored my words and failed to reach out to me until now, and you ignored Rikar's summon."

An icy river flowed down Talis's spine at the sorcerer's words. Aurellia was vile and revolting and intriguing at the same time. His nostrils flared and his eyes fired up with flecks of gold burning inside his irises.

"Now you are here, on this middling planet, the place of no cause, a step on the path towards home." Aurellia spread his arms like the unfolding of dragon's wings. "The world of shadows.

"You have come to save her, and now she is yours, and yet you are trapped here on this forsaken world. What will you do? Hmm... Your city has fallen to the Jiserians, Viceroy Lei is a traitor. There is nothing left for you back there. Look to the future!"

Talis clenched up his fists and fought the urge to strike out against him.

"Your family may well already be slain, the eradication of House Storm. There is deep enmity between your father and Viceroy Lei, did you not know this? Old rivals in the war for the heart. If you did ever manage to return home, what would you find? Tears and wailing and the gnashing of teeth?"

"I would find my city and my home." Talis glared at Aurellia. "Where is your home, old sorcerer?"

"Aye, I am old, as old as the sands of time. You are but a wink in that ebb and flow of light and shadows." Aurellia aimed a finger at the sky. "My home is far from here, far away amidst the stars of the night sky, where the glint of diamonds take their rest in the dark. A land of beauty and contrast, the soft light of the twin suns, the pale glow of the twin moons, a world of perfect balance, unlike your hideous world."

"Then why are you still here on this planet?" Talis chuckled. "Are you trapped like before? Bound to serve your time for thousands of years until a boy discovers the secret you so desperately need?"

"Ah, yes, your discovery was most fortunate, I thank you for that." The sorcerer leaned in close until Talis could see the hairs springing out from the mole on his face. "And from what I've heard, you have the Goddess Nacrea's ear, she listened to you. Why is that?"

"My prayer was sincere, my need was great. And I obeyed her and built a new Temple of the Sun, and planted the black crystal she gave me." Talis pictured the roaring flames of the temple beams and felt the anger bubbling up inside. "But they destroyed that beautiful temple, why did they destroy it?"

"They don't understand you, they don't understand the gods, your pitiful Order of the Dawn." Aurellia clapped his hands and curled his lips into a withered smile. "Enough talk of the past, let's talk of the future, shall we? I have a proposal for you, if you are interested in leaving this dreary land."

"What's that?" Talis said, recognizing the greed in Aurellia's eyes.

"Look to your map, you'll see Rikar. Prove your worth by making it here alive, then we will talk. If you ever try to summon my image again on the map, you will wish you were never born."

With that Aurellia vanished and the vision faded. Talis stared at the map and saw a point where Rikar was, far to the east, amidst mountains, and Aurellia waiting there for them... Was this all just another test? Talis glanced around at the smoldering flames issuing puffs of smoke into the sky, a certainty sinking into his bones. They really didn't have any other choice but to go out there and find them...

Charna pressed herself under Talis's arm and nuzzled his hand. He scratched her chin and under her ears, and she purred and murmured in response.

"Did you have a vision?" Mara said, her eyes blinking rapidly.

Talis still pictured Aurellia's hideous face. "It was him all along...the grand puppet-master. We're just pawns in his game."

Nikulo wrinkled up his face and coughed from the smoke. Talis told them his vision, and Mara frowned and her eyes sank as if absorbed in thought.

"He's tempting us and testing us at the same time," Talis said. "I imagine we have no choice but to play along."

"There's something I didn't tell you." Mara's face was pale and trembled slightly. "The sorcerer told me he obeys Aurellia and yet despises him at the same time. He said it was Aurellia that brought the downfall of Urgar, the City of Light, and with it the ancient Temple of the Sun. A group of ancients moved the Temple to the secret location where we found it, in order to hide it from Aurellia."

"So we betrayed them?" Talis said.

"No, Rikar betrayed us. It was he who was secretly communicating to Aurellia all along." Mara sighed. "Palarian said Aurellia needs only one more leap, one more jump through a World's Portal in order to reach their home world, the place where most of the ancients escaped after the war between Urgar and Darkov many thousands of years ago.

"But if that happens, the sorcerer said it would mean war and disaster on their home planet, not just a war of the immortals, but a war amongst the gods."

18

The Way of Shadows

As they trekked east the next morning towards the spiny grey mountains, images of the gods devastating Master Viridian flashed in Talis's mind. The shadow gods wrath striking so severely at such a minor offense... A war of the gods, the dark gods against the gods of light? If a student of Light Magic had to study Shadow Magic in order to avoid going insane, that meant worshipping different sets of gods, some light and some dark. What was he going to do?

Talis remembered Zagros and his host of nether-beasts and his army of risen dead. Would the God of the Underworld prevail against the Goddess Nacrea, Mistress of the Light? Charna came prancing up alongside and gave out a quick cry for attention. He scratched her between the ears and she purred in response, her golden eyes beaming in affection.

Nikulo pointed at a great wall off in the distance. "Doesn't look like we can go around it, and the main gates are well fortified."

"Aurellia won't make it easy for us to enter through the front gates, I'd say that's a losing proposition." Talis knew there had to be another way inside.

A distant storm flashed high amidst the jagged mountain peaks, and while they hiked through scattered scrub-brush, a cold wind whipped up and blasted dust into their eyes. They veered to the left and away from the main gates, down a dry gully littered with boulders and brush. Talis climbed along the gully towards the wall, all the while keeping an eye out for lookout towers and archers at the top.

Then Mara spotted an iron grating where the gully went under the wall. They stalked through the gully, hiding behind boulders strewn along the way, glancing up to see if they'd attracted any attention. The wall was at least a hundred feet tall and formed of seamless hewn stones. Talis carried Charna and whispered in her ear to be still.

Nikulo opened his mouth to talk, but Talis raised a finger to keep him quiet. He motioned towards the iron grating and kept an eye on the rim of the upper wall. The stone wall felt cool on his back as he set Charna down, and withdrew a flask of water and took a drink.

"Stay close," he said to Charna.

"There's nobody up there," whispered Nikulo. "Imagine how many men you'd need along such a vast wall?"

Talis bobbed his head in agreement and handed the flask to Mara. "What do you suppose is inside?"

Mara took a drink and shielded her eyes from the sun as she stared through the iron bars. "It looks like it tunnels down into the earth for awhile...it's pitch dark."

"Nominal security." Nikulo squeezed himself under the grating and grinned at them from the other side.

"Wait!" Talis hissed, and withdrew the Surineda Map. "Always be suspicious when they make it too easy."

Nikulo shrugged. "Simple laws of physics. When they built this the iron bars reached down into the ground. They've had quite a few floods here since then and the water has eaten away at the ground."

"Still, I trust Aurellia would have fortified any weaknesses into his domain." Talis closed his eyes and focused his mind on revealing any dangers nearby. The map burned in his hands, and when he opened his eyes, it was filled with symbols of death and poison and fire.

"The way is littered with magical wards," Talis said. He called Charna and bent down to whisper in her ears. "You have to stay close to me, the way is very dangerous ahead."

Nikulo backed up against the bars, fear blossoming in his eyes. "I'll let you lead."

"In fact, if you'd squeezed through a few feet to the left, you probably would have ignited in flames."

Mara peered at the map and wrinkled up her forehead. "I hope we can avoid all those traps."

"We'll need to keep together. Follow my lead." Talis bent down and slid under the sharp bars and raised the map close to his face. He stepped forward twenty paces, then went sideways until his head grazed the curving stone ceiling. *Clear for a stretch*, he thought, studying the map. He tiptoed forward, tripping over rocks and debris from the last flood.

"I can't see a thing," Mara said, and bumped into Talis.

"Would any of the magical wards be sensitive to light?" Nikulo said.

"I don't think we should risk casting any spells." The map emitted enough golden light for Talis to see where they were going. They crept along for what seemed like an hour, descending deeper into the earth, zigzagging around danger.

Nikulo groaned.

"What is it now?" Talis said.

"I...I have to go to the bathroom."

"Are you kidding me? Why didn't you go outside?" Mara said.

"I didn't want to be shot in the arse by an archer." Nikulo coughed and fidgeted back and forth.

Talis chuckled and pulled Mara's hand. "Go ahead, we'll wait farther up for you. Just follow the wall straight ahead, it's pretty safe around here."

"Can you guys plug your ears?"

"No...no you're not going to do it here? That's disgusting." Talis shuddered, unable to stop himself from imagining the hideous smell.

"I can't help it! When the urge comes, I can't stop it, can I?"

Talis grimaced and walked with Mara down as far as he could away from Nikulo. "We better cover our ears and noses."

"Is it that bad?" Mara whispered.

Even though Talis had plugged up his ears, he still heard groans and explosions and exclamations echo down the tunnel. The enemy surely heard all that noise, unless they were deaf. Then the smell came. Despite having squeezed his nostrils shut, the vile smell of rotten eggs and festering wounds leeched into Talis's mouth. He sneezed so hard snot flew out and splattered the map, causing it to dim slightly.

"That's so gross!" Mara yelled. "Gods...what a wretched smell!"

"All finished down here," Nikulo shouted, and Talis could hear the scraping sound of boots kicking stones and debris. Nikulo stumbled towards them.

Talis wiped the map with his shirt sleeve and froze when he noticed hundreds of tiny red dots moving towards them from behind Nikulo.

"Your shat was so loud it woke something nasty," Talis said, "and it's coming towards us."

Nikulo rammed into Talis and sent them tumbling across the ground. Charna hissed in response, her golden eyes glowing in the dark. Talis scooped up the map and listened to the chittering and squeaking and the scampering of thousands of little feet echoing down the tunnel. When the hundreds of glowing yellow eyes descended in the darkness, Talis sent a wave of flame down the tunnel, igniting the carpet of rats.

As the rats burned, the flames sent flickering shadows down the way, revealing the bones of those who had failed to travel through here before. But more rats came, leaping over their burning brothers and sisters, intent on assailing the intruders. Talis sent a massive burst of wind, knocking the second wave of rats back and into the whipped up rat fire.

The burning, smoky stench was horrific, and as hard as it was to imagine, worse than Nikulo's. The rats had to be diseased because the air was filled with the smell of rotting flesh and sickness, like a pile of burning plagued bodies.

"Let's get out of here!" Talis yelled, and coughed hard into his arm. He sent more wind down the tunnel to cast away the smell. The flames burst up higher behind them as they stumbled off.

Talis studied the Surineda Map for areas of danger ahead. "Keep an eye behind us and yell if they come close."

"I'll handle them," Nikulo said. "Just keep us moving!"

They dodged wards and pits and traps lodged in the floor. The tunnel was one enormous disaster. Talis heard Nikulo shoot off a hissing blast that sounded like the poison spell he'd used on the snakes.

"They're not affected by the poison," shouted Nikulo.

Talis turned, waited for Nikulo and Mara to stand behind, and concentrated on sending heat inside all the creatures below. Thousands of pops and miniature bloody explosions echoed down the tunnel, like corn popping on a pan over the fire.

"That's sick!" Mara said, covering her eyes. "I really didn't need to see that."

The last attack had an unintended desirable outcome. More rats scampered down the tunnel, but this time they stopped to feast on what was left of the cooked rats. Talis raced ahead, avoiding danger, and finally caught a glimpse of a faint light ahead. He held Charna back as they approached the iron bars on the other side of the tunnel.

"There are magical wards all along the exit." Talis stared at the Surineda Map. "How are we going to get around it?"

"Can you toss a rock or something to set the ward off?" Mara said.

Talis shook his head. "I doubt that would work, I don't even think the rats set off the wards. Probably they were set to only go off for humans."

"So there's no way through unless one of us sets off a ward?" Nikulo said, and frowned.

"Yes, exactly. But whoever went through the wards would be killed."

"That's terrible," Mara said. "We'll just go back and find another way inside."

"Wait, let's investigate. Follow me." Talis strode towards the iron bars, and stopped ten feet before the place where the wards were set.

"So the other side of the bars is all clear as far as I can see. But the wards are set right under the bars, so to get past you'd have to activate one of the wards." Talis studied the map again and realized that one of the wards was Fire Magic, the one along the left side.

"I have an idea." Talis put the map in his backpack and set it on the ground.

"What is it?" Mara said, doubt and fear creeping into her eyes. "You're not going to—"

"It probably won't hurt me... Don't be like that, I'm not going to get killed. I said I had an idea. Master Grimelore taught me an exercise of drawing in heat from a fire and holding it inside my body, then releasing it. I might be able to do the same thing here."

"Wait, let me see if I have your idiotic plan right." Nikulo grunted and wagged his head. "You're going to step on the flaming ward of death and instantly channel the energy out through a Fire Magic spell?"

"That's basically it. You have a better idea?"

"As a matter of fact, I do. And it's not just because it's my idea, it's because I'd rather not see you get roasted like those rats. That's what friends do, keep each other from getting killed."

"Well, what is it?" Mara said.

"Grab one of those handy portal runes you have. Open a portal to go as far away past those bars as you can see clearly."

"But I thought we could only open a portal and go to places we've been to before?" Talis said, but already he wondered if Nikulo was right.

"Palarian said that as a way of talking, but he never said a thing about line of sight. And I think it will work, as long as you can see the place of your destination clearly. For instance, I doubt you could go as far as those distant mountains, well you could, but you might end up inside the mountains, or say hundreds of feet above them... You get the idea."

It made perfect sense, and Talis wondered why he hadn't thought about it. Being at a place was as much seeing it as anything else. So Talis squinted as he stared outside, and fixed his gaze on an old scraggly pine tilting over sideways. A long spindly shadow was cast off to the right of the tree. A perfect place for porting to.

He placed the rune on the ground, pictured the shadow beside the pine tree, and cast the binding. The churning shadow portal formed in the tunnel, and they all jumped inside.

19

The Illusionist

Instead of stepping out from the portal onto the shadow of the pine, Talis found himself inches from the pine tree trunk itself. At least he wasn't *inside* the pine. His friends bundled up behind him, and Charna dove under the branches and scouted out ahead.

"Next time, maybe aim for something else other than a tree." Nikulo grunted as he bent down and made his way out from under the branches.

Talis glanced back at the great wall and realized from this vantage point that the wall wasn't manned at all, at least not along this stretch. He swiveled around and stared at the menacing mountains looming off in the distance. Aurellia and Palarian were there, waiting for them. And Rikar, what had happened to him?

Charna had caught a scent and dashed off east towards a thick patch of brush. They crept towards the bushes, mindful of any patrols that might be about. But the area around was wild and desolate and Talis doubted soldiers would bother defending around here. Considering all the wards and rats in the tunnel, most likely any soldiers would assume this part of the wall was impenetrable.

They hiked across the chaparral, then climbed over boulders and trekked up the high steppes leading towards the stormy mountains. Now the sky was silver and black, and the air smelled of storm and sage and pine. They were getting closer now, as Talis realized by plotting the way with the Surineda Map. Nestled high in the mountains lay a massive multi-layered castle surrounded by ramparts and fortifications.

Here they saw a pack of elk startled by the first patrols marching in formation: soldiers wielding short, curved blades, and wearing blood-red scale-and-bone armor. Talis, Mara, and Nikulo lay hidden beneath a large scrub brush, spying the movements of the troops.

"Where do you think our best approach to the castle is?" Nikulo whispered.

"Maybe down that gully to the left." Talis checked the map. "A bit of a climb up the rocks, but I think we can do it, especially with all your new climbing skills."

Nikulo grinned. "I was thinking the same thing."

"But what about any archers that might be up there above the rocks?" Mara said. "Why not take our time and head to the right through that forest over there, it would provide us with a lot more cover."

Talis and Nikulo looked at each and shrugged. "Valid point," Nikulo said. "And I hate getting shot in the face with an arrow."

"I bet you would." Mara scoffed, and wrinkled up her face. "So I take it we're heading around to the forest. I'll scout ahead and keep a lookout for patrols."

They had to cross under a stone bridge with soldiers tramping above as they marched in formation. A spindly river spidered down the mountainside with tufts of grass lining the edges. The day was dying by the time they reached the forest's edge, and the sky off to the west held a luminous orange wash.

In the twilight air the fragrance of juniper and pine and meat smoke wafted into Talis's nostrils. His stomach complained at the smell. The pine needle floor was soft under his footsteps, and Talis imagined it would make a fine resting place for the night. If they had a roasted hare or deer for supper, then the day would be complete. But Talis knew they'd probably go hungry for tonight as their supplies were gone along with the mules.

Mara slowed her ascent through the forest and pointed ahead at a flickering firelight splashing shadows across the tree trunks. Talis sidled up alongside her, and she whispered in his ear.

"A band of odd warriors. They seem disinterested in the surroundings, and overly fascinated with perfecting their roasted pig."

"Sounds like my idea of fun," Talis muttered. His mouth watered at the smell.

Nikulo waddled close and flicked his eyes in the direction of the campfire. "We have the advantage for a surprise attack, and the prize is a fine roast." He studied the camp. "And if my eyes aren't fooled by the distance, bottles of wine to go with it."

Talis peeked around a trunk and discovered that *odd* didn't begin to describe the warriors. They were a group of four, each one different than the other. The old, haggard looking warrior worshipping the roast was clad in wolf skin and wore an unkempt beard. He wielded a massive, jagged-edge hunting knife and looked ready to do battle with the oiled and crisped pig.

A young woman hovered over the fire, warming her hands as she smiled shrewdly at the bearded man beginning to carve the roast. She was dressed in a scarlet tunic, cut revealingly low in the front, and tied around the waist by what looked like a belt of thorns. Her long, charcoal hair was cinched up in a twirl by a thin twisted blade.

"The air smells foreign tonight," the woman said.

The bearded man frowned. "I used sprigs of new herb buds from the crags."

"She doesn't mean the roast," said a muscular baby-faced man with bushy blue hair. He wore white bone breastplate armor, and sat on a rock, removing bone leggings and wrist-guards.

An aged hermit-looking man dressed in a tattered brown cloak lay leaning against a log, his eyes only open a sliver. From what Talis guessed, he was either gazing at the fire or asleep. But for some reason Talis felt the man was aware of everything that was going on in his surroundings.

The listless air suddenly snapped to attention, swirled and gusted behind Talis, and sent the campfire blazing with pops and crackles and a shower of sparks flying towards the trees.

"We have guests," the hermit said, still keeping his eyes only open a sliver. Talis's heart thudded ahead an extra few beats when he realized the warriors knew they were there.

"Yes, yes, a foreign smell. The master said to expect company." The bearded man turned the roast, and sliced a few pieces of pig onto a platter. "Come, guests, share in our wine and roast."

Talis and Mara stared questioningly at each other, unsure of how to proceed.

"Don't be shy, we aim you no harm...at least during supper." The young woman grinned maliciously. "We like to feed our enemies first."

"Are they trying to bait us out into the open?" whispered Mara.

"Well, we've definitely lost the element of surprise." Nikulo frowned. "Besides, I'm hungry. Can't we fight them *after* we've eaten? They did offer."

Talis stared at the roast and felt his stomach grumble. "Is your master Aurellia?" Talis shouted.

Mara sent Talis a surprised look. "You just gave us away!" she hissed.

But the warriors by the fire remained unmoved. The old hermit stirred a bit, and said, "He is known by many names, and that is an old name he uses to those he tempts.

But you are out of his favor and he doubts your virtue. Come and eat and drink, we mean only to ask you questions. Depending on how you answer will shape our response."

Talis strode forward into the light, shaking off Mara's grasp. He narrowed his eyes at the old hermit, and ignored the cold stares of the other warriors.

"How did you know we were out there?" Talis said.

The old hermit sniffed. "Our senses are highly tuned to changes happening in the environment around us. Whether a doe or a squirrel or two boys and a young girl of a similar age. Your other friends are shy or simply disagreed with the idea of showing themselves? If you had tried to remain hidden, we would have simply hunted you down."

"Carax, perhaps that's what they wanted," said the young woman. She sent Talis a look that dared him to start a fight.

"You intended to assault us?" Carax said, his face amused. "You'll have to do better than that. Come sit, the roast is ready. And I can hear your other friend's stomach rumbling. Our swords are sheathed, we won't bring violence over a good meal."

Talis approached the fire and sat cautiously opposite Carax and the young woman. He nodded in appreciation as the old hermit handed him the platter of roasted pork. It tasted delicious, better than anything he'd had on this adventure. A cup of deep-red wine washed down the roast just fine.

"I'll have some roast if you're still offering," Nikulo said. He strode across the forest floor, glancing cautiously at the warriors. Mara followed, a vivid look of disdain on her face.

Talis offered them the pork platter, and felt relieved at Nikulo's thankful smile.

"Welcome, shy friends," Carax said, spreading his arms wide. "Time for us to parlay. I would know of your journey and know of you. The truth is best, I sniff lies like a hound sniffs the fox."

So Talis told them of the old sorcerer, and how Mara was kidnapped, and the journey thus far. Carax scowled when he heard the bits about Palarian.

"That foul old dog." Carax spat into the fire. "Caring more about his own skin than anyone else. Don't get me wrong, I can't blame him, being stuck on that world of yours for thousands of years, I'd want to go home as well."

The old hermit leaned forward and peered into Nikulo's eyes. "And just how long have you been poisoned?"

"How can you tell?" Nikulo looked taken aback. "It's been six months now."

"Hmm. You don't have long now, maybe a week left. First comes fatigue, then the sweats, and finally the convulsions and death. I'm sorry. If you like I can ask Adwina to end it for you."

The young woman chortled. "Maybe your end will come sooner than you think."

"Not until they've finished their supper," the bearded man said, and scowled at Adwina. "I will not have my pork roast disrespected. On a full stomach they'll make much finer opponents."

"So then we'll fight after dinner?" Mara said, narrowing her eyes at the bearded man.

"Spar is a much better word. You have such a concept on your world?"

Talis thought of the intense battles that took place in the training arenas. "We do, with a healer watching—"

"But sometimes people die," Mara said, interrupting him. "And we're not allowed to use magic."

Carax chuckled. "No magic? What a ridiculous system. Rules for the rigid rabble-rousers. What are our rules, Tenuva?"

The young man with the blue hair allowed a grin to spread across his face. "Rules? Only one, you must fight. And how long must you fight? Until your opponent is dead. So eat and enjoy the roast, I'm looking forward to killing all of you."

Nikulo raised a glass of wine to the young man. "I'll drink to that. But did you hear that blue-haired bastards have weak minds?" He dug two fingers into his temple and clenched his jaw as he stared at Tenuva. The young man writhed around, slapping at his own head until his eyes flipped back in his sockets and drool rolled out of his slack mouth.

"Tsk, tsk," the old hermit said. "I suppose dinner is finished."

The bearded man swung his hunting knife around and let it plunge into the heart of the blue-haired boy, who gasped one last time and fell into the fire, flames lapping around his head.

Mara jerked her wrist and threw a dagger at Adwina, but the weapon pinged off scales that had formed instantly from her neck down to her ankles. Adwina cartwheeled over the fire and slammed spiked-laden feet into the ground where Mara had once stood. Talis spun his hands around and shot a burst of wind, sending the scaly-skinned woman bouncing off tree trunks back into the darkness.

The old hermit flew up his hands and his tattered robe flapped back as ice shards shot from his palms, his face a hideous contortion of rage and mockery. Talis reacted just in time, issuing a hundred tendrils of flame from his fingertips to melt the ice, and only a gush of water remained to eradicate the campfire in a burst of smoky haze.

Talis pulled Mara and Nikulo back to hide in the shadows, but the bearded man circled around the mist and followed them in big, noisy stomps, stabbing tree trunks with his hunting knife along the way.

"I'm going to rip my roasted pork right from your belly."

Nikulo grunted. "I like my belly just the way it is, thank you." He aimed his gaze at the bearded man, fingers on his temple, and the warrior stopped in his charge.

Then the world blinked, flashing yellow and silver lights, and the forest disappeared. Talis found himself alone in a desert at the bottom of a massive sand dune, with the wind whipping sand particles from the tip of the dune.

"What's going on?" Talis shouted, and spun around to find metallic gold spiders chattering towards him. Was this some kind of an illusion?

"Mara!" He raised his hands to cast Fire Magic at the spiders now only a few feet away. Flames burst out from his fingertips and scorched the sand, but the spiders just bowed down and were unaffected by the flames. He tried Wind Magic and the spiders flipped back and landed crouched, then continued their advance despite the terrific gale.

He realized this indeed was an illusion, and rather than wasting his power fighting the spiders, cast Wind Magic against the ground and propelled himself up and back a hundred feet until landing at the top of the dune. The spiders wavered away, as if a mirage broken, but farther out in the endless dunes something enormous was rolling towards him, a beast surrounded by a violent sand storm.

A sudden fear stuck Talis: if this was his illusion then wasn't his body now at risk of being slain? How could he break the illusion? He thought back to his magical training dreams, and all that Master Viridian had taught him, and he remembered something. *When a nightmare possesses you, wake up in your dream, and realize it is not real. Focus on one thing in your dream and the dream will either change or end.*

So Talis focused his magical power on his gaze, and stared at the ground and soon the illusion wavered and shimmered and changed back to the dark forest.

Adwina stood over Mara, scales still covering the young woman, her twisted blade thrust out towards Mara's neck.

20

The Castle

Talis remained still, determined to save Mara, and focused fire energy into Adwina's heart. The young woman's eyes went wild as she clenched her chest, then darkened into a blank gaze. Talis felt a sick knot tighten his stomach as she fell silently to the side, an angry stain of red dribbling from her delicate mouth.

Mara lay lost in a nightmare, her eyelids fluttering, oblivious to Adwina's assault. He had to find the illusionist, but quietly, without the old hermit knowing he was released from the dream.

Talis pretended he was caught in a fitful sleep, but all the while through barely opened eyes he scanned the forest, searching for Carax. Beneath a stump lay Nikulo, kicking and twitching, and the bearded man stood obediently nearby, still locked under the mind control spell that Nikulo had cast.

Talis pushed himself up, stalked around, and hid behind a tree once he found what he was searching for. Past the stump, brilliant emerald eyes pierced the dark, the eyes of the illusionist, the eyes conjuring the nightmares.

Talis gaped at the radiating waves of energy pouring out from the old hermit.

How would he stop Carax? A direct assault might just throw Talis into another nightmare and give the illusionist the extra time needed to revive the bearded man from Nikulo's spell. Talis had a feeling the old hermit had forged a kind of magical protection as his shield, to keep him from harm's way. The air around the illusionist shimmered.

Then Charna stalked up close to Talis, her golden eyes bobbing in the blackness. She murmured and nuzzled against his chin.

"Good girl," Talis whispered. "We've got to stop that man." He pointed at the illusionist. If Charna could create a distraction, Talis could try breaking through his defense. He withdrew his father's sword, and felt the heat rush up his arm and swirl through his body.

Talis stalked from tree to tree, keeping his gaze locked on Carax's green eyes. The illusionist was seemingly lost in his own illusions, and paid little attention to anything around. When they were positioned behind the old hermit and close enough to kill, Talis sent Charna after Carax and circled around to the right.

The illusionist flung his hands up and jumped as Charna sunk her teeth into his calf. He tried to kick her off, but she just dug in harder until the old hermit howled in pain. Talis leapt forward and stabbed his sword down at the illusionist's back. Carax twisted around just as the blade was about to strike, and Talis felt himself launched into the air, floating away from the old man. Talis flung the blade at the man's chest, but the illusionist just swept it aside with the slightest gesture of his finger. Carax aimed a hand at Charna and the lynx fell asleep.

"You thought you could murder me with a cat and a blade?" The old hermit chuckled. "How did you break out of the trap I spun for you? Oh, you've such hateful eyes... Go ahead, cast your devastating spell on me, what are you afraid of? Or is there a reason you chose a blade rather than a spell?"

There was a reason Talis chose the blade, he could see clearly now the glowing shield around Carax's body. The illusionist was protected by a kind of energy shield, perhaps one that resisted magical attacks? Or even worse, what if that was a mirror shield and sent magic back onto the caster? But the shield did nothing against Charna's teeth. If they were to defeat the illusionist, somehow it had to be done with steel.

After the shift of the old hermit's attention, Talis spotted Nikulo and Mara through a break in the trees stalking towards them, and sighed in relief, realizing the fight must have broken the illusionist's spell.

"Why should such a powerful illusionist as yourself need to do Aurellia's bidding?" Talis knew he had to keep Carax distracted long enough for Mara and Nikulo to attack.

The illusionist scoffed. "You call this power? I'm no fool with an overinflated ego, I know true magical genius when I see it."

"So you're loyal to Aurellia because of what?"

"To learn, you fool. You would be wise to value that above all things in life. A wise master can teach you many things, like for instance the heightened awareness that your friends are trying to sneak up on me." Carax snapped his fingers twice and Mara and Nikulo slumped to the ground.

"Yes, I know this and much more. Your pet caught me off guard, she's no ordinary creature... Tell me, before I kill you, where did you find this magnificent cat?"

Talis clenched his jaw, his mind racing, trying to think of way to defeat the illusionist or at least to protect himself against his power. "Charna is a gift from the Goddess Nacrea."

"The Goddess Nacrea? Don't be ridiculous—"

A blinding light suddenly vaporized the blackness of the forest and the illusionist cried out in agony. Talis suddenly found himself plummeting towards the ground, and pain shot through his body as he slammed onto the pine needle floor. Stars spun in his eyes and he wheezed, unable to take a breath. What had just happened? Talis craned his neck around, trying to find the illusionist. He pushed himself up to his knees, watching the golden light swirling in the air, forming a face that Talis thought looked like the Goddess Nacrea. He reached out, trying to touch a fragment of the Goddess, but found the light slowly fade from the sky.

Darkness returned as a thick blanket, so Talis cast a small orb of Light Magic and let it float into the air, sending shadows slithering across the forest. The illusionist had vanished. Or perhaps something far worse. The gruesome image of Master Viridian being savaged by the gods played over in his mind's eye. Now he knew that the Goddess Nacrea had struck Carax down. Talis gazed at Charna when she shook her head and peered wisely into his eyes.

"You truly are a gift from the Goddess Nacrea." Talis raised his eyes to the sky and sent the Goddess his deepest thanks for saving them.

Mara and Nikulo slowly stirred, groggy, shaking their heads, eyes blurry and wondering.

"What happened?" Nikulo said, his voice deep and slurred.

"Carax sensed you stalking him." Talis snapped his finger. "That was all he had to do to stop you. He just focused his mind on making you sleep, and that was it."

Nikulo's eyes were deep in thought. "My master could do such a thing, though not nearly with such ease or with such force. He taught me over the last few months how to gain a greater hold over controlling people."

"I've noticed." Talis glanced at the bearded man still standing and slobbering, eyes blank, waiting for Nikulo's command.

"This one's mind was particularly easy once I burrowed my way through his defenses. I'm surprised the spell hasn't broken yet." Nikulo tapped the bearded man on the forehead. "What secrets locked inside would you like to share with us?"

Mara nudged Talis and tucked herself close to him. He wrapped his arm around her and realized she was freezing.

"Let's go by the fire and warm up," Talis said.

Nikulo commanded the bearded man-zombie to follow them, and plopped down next to the smoldering campfire. Talis added more wood to the fire, and stoked it up hot. He cast a small amount of fire energy inside Mara's body until she warmed, her cheeks turning pink.

"Feeling better?" Talis touched her forehead and felt tiny drops of perspiration.

She smiled appreciatively, her face an expression of admiration and warmth. "So how did you defeat Carax?"

"I didn't. The Goddess Nacrea struck the illusionist when he doubted Charna was a gift from the Goddess. She saved us…."

Mara's eyes had widened when Talis told her the story, and now she cuddled up even closer until Talis felt tingles erupt across his skin where she touched him. She looked fondly up at his eyes and nuzzled his neck with her lips.

"Time to question our chubby zombie." Nikulo aimed his eyes at the bearded man. "What's the best way to sneak inside the castle?"

The bearded man's mouth flopped open, and a line of drool dribbled out.

"Let me release him halfway from the spell," Nikulo said. The bearded man's jaw twitched a bit and his eyes blinked rapidly, tears streaming down his face. He glanced up at Nikulo as if fearful of being struck.

"Can you understand me?" Nikulo bent down and stared at the man's face.

The bearded man kept his eyes low. "I understand."

"Good, that's better. Now tell us how to sneak into the castle."

"There are guards everywhere, constantly on patrol—ahh, no, that hurts!"

"I didn't ask that, I asked how to sneak inside. Focus."

"The sewer...I know an unguarded entrance through the sewers." The bearded man grimaced and twisted up his face, like he was trying to fight Nikulo's hold over his mind.

Nikulo puckered up his lips and nodded in satisfaction. "Take us there."

The pine forest swept up the mountain until it reached a wall of boulders and bluffs, with the many-layered castle towering high above. They followed the wet stench up through the boulders and into a cave that sloped up into the heart of the mountain. Either side of the cave floor was thankfully dry, but the middle held a slow running river of filthy sludge.

Talis unfurled the Surineda Map and discovered the way was free of traps (other than occasional smelly mounds of surprise). He signaled Nikulo to continue their ascent inside and cast a sphere of golden light to guide their way.

"Can't you summon a spell to take the stench away?" Nikulo's voice sounded nasally as he'd pinched his nostrils together.

"We've smelled worse in the Underworld." Mara frowned as if remembering the hideous scene.

Far ahead they discovered steps snaking up, and the bearded man motioned for them to follow the way up into the darkness. Talis treaded cautiously as the steps wound up and around, finally depositing them into a cellar filled with potatoes and onions and garlic. At the other side of the room, an iron door allowed faint light from the outside through its bars.

"I don't suppose you have the key," Nikulo said to the bearded man. "No?"

Talis inspected the lock and found it a simple contraption. He sent fire energy into the area around the lock mechanism and the metal glowed white hot until the lock snapped and the door swung open.

"Do we need him anymore?" Mara said.

Nikulo shook his head and commanded the bearded man back to the forest. The man shambled off towards the sewers and disappeared into the darkness.

"What are we going to do when we find Aurellia?" Nikulo said.

"We talk to him." Talis felt an eye twitch and he rubbed a hand across his face. "He said he had a way for us to get off this planet."

"This is one enormous trap we're walking into," Mara said.

"Do you have any other ideas? No? Then I don't either. I do know I'd rather sneak in unannounced than fight my way in." Talis studied Nikulo, noticing a change in his friend. "What's wrong?"

"I hope there's a cure for my poison. I'm starting to feel something weakening me."

"Really?" Mara said, placing a hand on his arm.

Nikulo brushed beads of sweat from his forehead. "I feel hot and clammy at the same time. Let's get out of here, this place is suffocating."

Talis cast a worried look at Nikulo, wondering what he could do to help. When they found Aurellia, Talis was determined to demand that the sorcerer cure Nikulo of his poison. They climbed the stairs up and around until the way opened up into an empty stone courtyard lined with arches and pillars. Talis made the golden orb disappear, and they crept along, keeping their backs to the wall. Charna padded alongside, sniffing the air.

Through a narrow corridor Talis could hear the clapping of boots against stone. He motioned for them to head down to the other side of the courtyard. The castle loomed higher in the distance.

"Do you think Aurellia is up there?" Mara whispered.

"I can't use the map to track him." Talis frowned, withdrawing the Surineda Map.

"Keep that out," Nikulo said. "It can help us navigate the castle and keep us from bumping into soldiers."

"And find Palarian or Rikar? Don't you think they'll be close to Aurellia?" Mara flashed Talis a knowing look.

Talis ran a finger across the map's surface, feeling the heat rush up his arm and warm his body. He focused his mind on finding Palarian and Rikar, sensing any danger from guards, and displaying all the rooms and corridors of the castle.

Rikar was nowhere to be found on the map.

The sorcerer was ahead at the main castle, although Talis couldn't tell if he was high above or deep below. The map was littered with spidery passageways criss-crossing atop the many levels of the castle.

"So confusing," Talis said. "Palarian is here, but I can't tell what level he's on."

Mara tilted her head, peering at the map. "Simple. Shift the perspective on the map to see it sideways."

She had a point. Talis commanded the map to show the castle from a side view, and there it was.

Palarian was down in the deepest depths of the castle dungeon.

21

The Dungeon

The Surineda Map displayed hundreds of red and orange and magenta points of light moving through the many layers of the castle. But where Palarian was down deep in the dungeon contained only magenta dots glowing eerily.

"I have a terrible feeling about going down there," Mara said, her voice shaky. "I told you this was all a trap. Why would Palarian be down there? Is he a prisoner?"

Talis frowned at the map, his hands trembling from the heat. "And why are there only magenta colored dots in the dungeon?"

"Ask the map if there's anything to eat and drink around here." Nikulo slapped his belly. "I'm hungry."

Mara rolled her eyes at Nikulo. "Didn't you just eat a few hours ago? You practically ravaged that roast."

"I'm guessing magenta dots are a bad thing indeed, and I'd rather not go into battle feeling hungry."

"Maybe there's a way we can avoid fighting," Talis said.

"You carrying a magic cloak of invisibility or something?" Nikulo scoffed.

"No, I wish. But if we simply avoid the dots, we're most likely to avoid fighting, right?"

Talis stared at the map again, trying to figure out how to navigate down to where Palarian was in the dungeon. They were on the ground level now, but the sorcerer was seven levels down in the lowest part of the castle. Talis imagined seeing the map at a top-down yet slightly rotated view, so he could make out two levels at a time. That was exactly what he wanted. With this view he could see all the stairwells and still keep an eye on the enemies walking around.

"Let's go." He grinned at Mara, proudly showing her the map.

"That's amazing!" she said, studying the map. "How did you get it like that? I've never seen a map drawn at an angle."

Nikulo peered over as well. "Maybe we can navigate the dungeon without being seen."

They stalked towards a side entrance leading down into the first level. The wooden door was old and ready to fall apart. This had to be the servant's entrance as Talis noticed dropped cabbage leaves and a shriveled potato on the grimy floor. The way down was dark, and the air smelled of garlic and roast.

"I do believe we found the kitchen," Nikulo whispered, and licked his lips.

The map displayed all orange dots in the next room, so Talis figured they were servants, and hopefully not a threat.

As they entered the room, fearful eyes glanced at them, then gazed at the floor. Talis pretended he was there to inspect the kitchen, keeping his back stiff and chin raised arrogantly.

"What's the garlic dish you're preparing? Ah…a pot of soup? A sample? Yes, of course, my friend here is hungry." Talis gestured towards Nikulo.

"Garlic cream soup?" Nikulo opened his mouth expectantly. "How do you make it?"

A tall, gangly man with thinning hair raised an eyebrow at Nikulo. "Sheep's cream, devil's garlic, black pepper, diced potatoes, shredded cabbage. And other assorted ingredients I'd prefer not to divulge."

"Devil's garlic? I'm not familiar with the term."

The cook motioned Nikulo over to an old, abused table filled with enormous garlic cloves tinged with a distinctive purplish hue. Nikulo inspected the garlic and sniffed curiously.

"Might I have a taste of the soup? Oh…well…if you insist I try a whole bowl, I certainly couldn't refuse. And bread? That's an interesting looking loaf…."

"Flatbread with rosemary." The cook studied Nikulo, and glanced at Charna, eying the lynx suspiciously. "Are you visitors of the master?"

"You could say that." Talis flashed the man an honest smile.

"Perhaps the other young master and young miss would enjoy a bite as well?"

205

Talis and Mara waved the idea away. "We've just eaten."

The other servants returned to their tasks: cleaning pots, kneading dough, cutting vegetables, hacking meat, and placing food on plates. Nikulo belched and massaged his stomach, a warm smile spreading across his face.

"A most excellent soup...my compliments to the cook. And a fine bread, too."

The cook bowed and the old woman kneading bread tilted her head and allowed a faint smile to lighten her worn face.

Talis motioned towards the far door, and Nikulo brushed off his hands and gave the soup bowl back to the cook. They were close to the door when the old woman cleared her throat.

"Such kind young masters," she said, her voice melodic and soft. "If only the other young masters were so kind...."

At her words Talis felt pity for these people, so fearful of the ruling house, and perhaps abused by the soldiers as well.

"Nice people," Mara whispered, and stepped through the door Talis held open.

"And fabulous cooks... You don't think we could hang around for supper?" Nikulo's eyes looked hopeful.

Talis shook his head, wishing there was more they could do to help them, but knew they were probably powerless in a direct fight against Aurellia and his army. He felt the tepid power flowing from the crystal in his backpack, and the truth sank deep inside: it wasn't enough power to win.

"Down here is another stairwell," Talis said. "I think this is the servant's way leading to the lower chambers. That should help us avoid well traveled areas."

They found it easy to sneak five levels down through stone corridors, past statues of gargoyles, angels, demons, and scowling figures of former masters of the house. The lower levels contained prison cells with shackles waiting to bind, iron bars flung open carelessly, and guards who marched as if they were the only ones here.

But once they reached the sixth level, after winding down and around a spiraling stone stairwell, they found a vast earthen chamber, dark and dank, with razor-sharp spikes pointing up, covering every inch of the floor.

"What in the name of Nyx?" Mara said, bending down to inspect a spike.

Talis huffed. "You'd need to fly to get across the room. Be careful, Charna, stay back here with us." He patted the lynx's head, and she murmured in response.

"Aurellia said he'd test us," Nikulo said. "How are we going to get past this?"

"We could tie boards on our feet," Mara said, and grinned.

"Somehow I have a feeling that wouldn't work." Talis glanced around the room and found a stone. He placed it on a spike and nodded as the stone was eaten away by the metal.

"Nasty," Mara said. "Magic infused in the spike?"

"I'm guessing even flying wouldn't get you safely to the other side either." Talis tossed a rock across the room, and the spikes shot up into the air and the stone exploded into dust.

Mara and Nikulo jumped at the explosion. "Maybe we can find another way back home," she said, her voice uncertain.

"I have a better idea." Talis summoned a brilliant golden orb and sent it across the room. Spikes shot up towards the orb, but retreated after doing nothing to harm the light. Far off on the other side of the room, the orb shone on a ledge in front of a stone door. Their destination. He bent down and placed a rune on the dry earth, pictured the ledge in his mind's eye, and cast a binding spell. The glowing rune characters illuminated the dust flittering in the air. He stepped on the rune and a churning shadow portal appeared, beckoning them inside.

"And you're sure that somehow the spikes won't get us?" Mara frowned.

"Well, they couldn't harm the orb… And I think technically we won't even be anywhere near the spikes." Talis rubbed his chin, hoping it was true. "I think one moment we'll be here and the next moment we'll be over there…."

Nikulo motioned Talis towards towards the shadow portal. "Then by all means…after you."

"What? You don't trust me? Oh, I get it, I'm the test subject."

"You could say that." Nikulo raised his hands, a doubtful expression on his face.

Talis exhaled sharply, upset that Nikulo expected him to go first. He stared into the portal and took a step forward, then finally decided to jump through.

The ledge where Talis landed was sloped down towards the spikes. He was about to turn and wave at Mara and Nikulo, to tell them it was safe, when he felt something pulling at his ankle.

A shadowy hand, snaking out from the portal, was dragging him back inside.

22

The Netherworld

Talis kicked at the shadowy hand, and cast Light Magic in powerful bursts, trying to break free of its grasp, but the thing soon yanked him back into the portal, inside a world of gloom.

Then the thing at his ankle was gone.

He raised his head from the ash-covered ground, trying to make sense of what he saw. The sky was pale like a bone, faint but still blanched white. The trees were the trees from his vision of Rikar, strange and alien, limbs red like blood-soaked blades, leaves listless and flapping in the whistling wind. And the banded bark on the trees was like scale-mail armor, as if the trees were warriors ready to swoop down and strike hordes of invaders.

But the land was barren and dry, silted remains of an ancient fire, as if from the bones of a vast army burned to ash. The remnants of sorrow. And the trees thrived from the pain, thrived from the nutrients of suffering, vivid and stark against the bleak land.

He smelled the coming of winter, of snow and ice and pine, and could feel the cold creep down into his skull. His ears tingled at the sharp wind gusting the ash into a whorl, stinging his eyes until tears dripped down his cheeks. There was a hissing sound, low and shrill, echoing off the trees, coming closer to where he knelt. His body tensed at the sound, waiting for something to strike.

Off in the distance, through the quavering dust, Talis glimpsed a cloaked figure strolling towards him. In quick successive shifts forward the figure now stood ten feet away, face obscured by the shadow of the hood.

"You made a mistake coming after me," Palarian said, his voice clear and sharp. "And you fell so easily into the trap set to bait you. I left the girl for you, why didn't you just leave and find another way home?"

"You kidnapped her!" Talis shouted, raising his hands to attack the sorcerer. "Why did you do that?"

"I had no choice." Palarian's wrinkled eyes pleaded with him. "You weren't exactly cooperative helping me leave your world. I had to find a way back home."

"And this is home?"

Palarian shook his head. "This is the proving land, the Netherworld, a land of shadows and pain. Home is one more step away."

"Your home...mine is back where I came from."

"You could have gone home with the girl instead of coming here."

"How could we? We had no crystal powerful enough to cast the spell."

The sorcerer wagged his finger at Talis. "But you had the map. You could have searched for a crystal! Why did you come here?"

Talis felt his heart drop down to his stomach. Why had he come here... And why didn't he think to use the map to find a crystal? He shouldn't have listened to Aurellia. There was nothing he had to tell him that would help find a way back home. Palarian was right, the answer lay with the Surineda Map. But he remembered, he didn't know the runes to get back home. Even with a powerful enough crystal he still couldn't open a portal to his world. His stomach clenched at the thought.

"You're here now, trapped in the Netherworld, like your old friend."

"Rikar is here?" The tortured vision flashed in Talis's mind.

"He's over there in those hills...in a cave, learning how to be earnest." A pitying frown crossed Palarian's face, as if he were really worried about Rikar.

"So there's no seventh level of the castle dungeon?"

The sorcerer spread his arms wide. "There is a seventh level. This place is something else entirely. You look perplexed...but that's alright, you don't need to understand everything. You're here, that's all that matters."

"I'm here trapped in Aurellia's web. What does he want with me, anyways?" Aurellia had Rikar as an apprentice, so why was Talis so important to him?

"You've royal blood…and the gods listen to you. Rikar is just another weapon for Aurellia, but you, having the gods' ear, well that just might change everything for Aurellia." Palarian swept off his hood, revealing his old, wrinkled face. "And you have the map. A map that only you can command. Remember? The gods gave it to you."

"How do you know that?"

"Your friend Mara told me. She's a gem, that one." The sorcerer allowed a smile to curve his lips up. "You should value her, cherish her…she cares for you a great deal."

Thinking of Mara made Talis worry about her stuck in the dungeon, with only Nikulo to help her. "Is she safe? Back in the dungeon?"

Palarian wagged his hands from side to side, as if uncertain. "She'll be fine…and well taken care of." His words sent a chill down Talis's spine as he realized Mara and Nikulo would soon be captured, and there was nothing he could do about it.

"If you treasure her, like I see in your eyes that you do, you should find a way home, and protect her."

"And you'll help me escape?" Talis said, his voice filled with disbelief.

A shrewd look cross the sorcerer's face. "Perhaps, perhaps."

"How can I trust you? You've already betrayed me."

"You have no other choice." Palarian chuckled, pushing himself up to his feet. "You're stuck here, in a world of Shadow Magic, where the rules are twisted, and where no other magic works." Talis clenched his face up. How could he escape if his magic didn't work here?

"But you said before that you didn't know Shadow Magic?"

"Hah, do you expect people to tell the truth? I've lived over thirteen-thousand years. How could I not know Shadow Magic? When you live that long you learn many things, things you wish you'd never learned."

Thirteen-thousand years? Talis gaped at the man, wondering about all that he'd seen and experienced during his life. What were the ancient kingdoms like? His imagination exploded, thinking of all the stories he'd read of history, of civilizations long ago, of people and places buried in the fabric of time. He held his tongue, despite wanting to ask Palarian a million questions.

"One day I'll share stories of times long gone, of better days and memories that harass your heart. I've seen it all, the proud City of Urgar crumbling under ten thousand dark spells and countless undead hordes, the creation of civilization on your planet, the very first spark! My father's eyes as he gazed at me, for the last time, hope passed into my heart, even as his enemies captured me and forced me to master their dark arts.

"These are the memories that plague the ancient mind. Of love and love lost. Of never returning to the place in time that felt like it would never go away. Immortal youth."

Palarian sighed and inhaled a great gulp of wind. "We were all banished to your planet, Aurellia and his followers, by those of our world, the world known to us as Vellia, our home, the world of shadows and light. A world of infinite beauty."

Talis could see the sorcerer caught in a rapturous picture, his face gleaming pure as a child's, as if he were there back home. Now he understood why Palarian did the things he'd done back in Naru. Talis was certain he would do anything to bring Mara and Nikulo back home. Did he even care about helping Rikar? Talis frowned, thinking Rikar probably didn't even want any help.

"By now your friends are in the comfort of the master's captivity." Palarian slapped his hands together and inky clouds formed, bubbling together in the air. "And I am tasked with your training. We'll see if you survive or go mad like many of the others."

"Training?" Talis scowled. "But I want to escape. You said—"

"I said perhaps. But my orders are to train you in the ways of Shadow Magic. And not the weak magic of the Jiserians you faced in battle. Light Magic is devastatingly brutal against such enemies, but powerless against what I'll be teaching you. Even if you possess a crystal given to you by a Goddess."

Talis was tempted to try and cast a shadow portal, thinking that it might work here, but he remembered the shadow hand that had dragged him here and thought he'd better not try. Palarian pushed the bubbling cloud out thousands of feet in front of him, through a hole in the eerie forest.

"This world is troublesome to walk across, so the first lesson is always travel. A Shadow Blink is a spell that lets you leap forward instantly across visible distances, as you could with your portal spell, but much faster and consuming less energy."

The sorcerer shook the inky cloud until it wound around and resolved down to a fibrous cord of black energy. "I'm showing you what is normally invisible. Here in the Netherworld shadow things are much more easily seen and controlled. I've shown you a shadow cord, billions of which exist throughout the universe. To cast the Shadow Blink spell you simply feel the shadow cords with your stomach and attach your own energy cords to the shadow ones, and the shadow cords pull you off to your destination."

Talis stared in horror and fascination at the area in front of Palarian's stomach. Hundreds of luminous living fibers stretched out from his robes, undulating, probing, until they attached to the shadow cord that stretched out for thousands of feet through the forest. The shadow cord bound itself to Palarian's fibers, and instantly the sorcerer blinked off into the distance. A moment later Palarian appeared back to where Talis gaped at the strange sight.

"Who needs to fly when you can do that?" The sorcerer's eyes crinkled up in amusement. "And if you do know how to fly"—Palarian soared twenty feet up into the air—"you fly so much faster." And he was gone again, and back in a flash.

"Now it's your turn."

How am I supposed to do that? Talis thought. Palarian picked up on his doubt and motioned him over to where he stood. "Breathe naturally, inhale by pushing your stomach out, and exhale slowly." With a quick strike, Palarian actually reached inside Talis's stomach and pulled a bundle of luminous cords out from within his body. Talis felt instantly sick to his stomach and fought the urge to vomit all over the sorcerer.

"What did you do?" Talis gaped at the fibers moving and stretching out from his own stomach. Were they there inside him all along, waiting to come out?

"I just removed the block in your mid-section, which prevented you from utilizing your own latent power." Palarian nodded in satisfaction, studying the fibers. "Your hands and fingers were open to the flow of magic, but your stomach was blocked."

"Blocked by what?"

"By birth and youth and foolishness." The old man grinned. "Now pay attention. Close your eyes and feel the fibers of your stomach."

Talis felt something itch along his stomach, whip around in front of his body, stretching out from within himself. He could feel it! Then a sickening sensation tickled over whatever he was feeling, and he opened his eyes in alarm.

"Good, you felt that." Palarian held a thick shadow cord that whipped about in the space surrounding Talis's mid-section. "Now close your eyes again and make your stomach fibers search out until you feel that same sensation...the shadow cords. When you feel it, grab it with your stomach and don't let go, no matter what you feel."

Despite wanting to run away and never feel that diseased sensation again, Talis did what the sorcerer asked. He concentrated on stretching the fibers out from his stomach until he felt the wet blackness seep into him. He fought down the nausea and allowed himself to grasp the black cord through his stomach's fibers. When he opened his eyes, Palarian nodded in approval.

"Excellent! I've never seen an apprentice perform the task so smoothly and without interruption from...unpleasantries. You've had some experience with shadow energies, I can tell."

Talis thought back to the shadow trap he'd built in the meadow with Mistress Cavares.

"Now let the shadow cord pull you along to your destination."

"But how do I summon a shadow cord?"

The sorcerer laughed with his eyes. "There is no summoning involved, shadow cords are simply everywhere in the universe. You just reach out with your stomach and concentrate on staring at your destination and use your willpower to go. It's quite simple."

A shadow flickered over the rocky hills to the right, distracting Talis for a moment. He completely forgot about his task and peered at the black spot, wondering if Rikar was there. The shadow cord snapped at his stomach, yanking him forward until the next second he was standing high atop the hills next to a cave's gaping mouth.

Palarian appeared next to him, flustered, a disapproving look in his eyes. "I said concentrate, that means not allowing yourself to get distracted." He glanced around then aimed his gaze at Talis. "Well at least you succeeded in performing your first Shadow Blink. What did you see here anyways?"

"A shadow...but it's not here anymore."

"You glimpsed a demon, most likely. Many live here within the cave."

"Is this where Rikar is studying?" Talis felt a hot sensation creep into his feet when he stared into the blackness of the cave.

"More like *enduring*, that's a better word. He's learning to withstand the corrupting influence of demonic powers, while slowly siphoning off their power."

Talis found his eyes widening. "Why would someone want to siphon off powers from a demon?"

"Ah...I see you've never understood how Shadow Magic works. You think of magic in terms of elemental magic, which uses stored power within the body, or from the outside, like a fire, or draws from a crystal that channels power. But Shadow Magic doesn't always require crystals or fire or heat from the body."

"What does it need?" Talis furrowed his brow, perplexed that he'd never wondered why the Jiserian sorcerers could travel so far away from their cities, and still be filled with power. He always assumed they carried crystals or some magical artifact with them.

Palarian spread his hands out and pinched the air. Shadow bubbles appeared around his fingers. "There are lines of shadow energy everywhere in the universe, waiting for the skilled sorcerer to draw in the power."

Power everywhere you went? "Then why can't Aurellia cast a world's portal spell without a powerful enough crystal?"

"There's not enough power available in any one place to draw from the shadow cords. Hence the need for demons, who naturally can store shadow energy within specific organs in their body."

"And crystals?"

"Yes, of course, the right crystal can channel vast amounts of magical energy."

"Channel?"

Palarian nodded his head. "Crystals don't store power, they channel it, and the most powerful crystals can draw in so much power it covers the distance of an entire world. Enough power to summon a world's portal spell, used to travel an immense distance across the stars."

"And those crystals are extremely rare."

"Precisely." The sorcerer gestured towards the cave. "So now we enter."

"Wait, if what you need can be only found through the Surineda Map, why don't you just have me find a crystal and your done?"

"Without having the ability to sense and draw in shadow energy, you'll most likely be unable to find such a crystal, even with the Surineda Map." Palarian strode towards the gaping mouth of the cave. "And demons always hide such a powerful crystal, so you must first conquer a demon stronger than the one used to destroy your Order's source of power."

23

Demon's Lair

Talis could feel the wickedness slowly seep into his mind, the thoughts and cravings of the twisted minds of demons. Hunger for flesh, the taste of warm blood, the fear and loathing and suspicion. They hid here away from the world, away from the brightness, clinging to pain, suffering in silence. And it festered and grew until rancid with hatred for life.

So this was where Rikar was being tortured? Talis wondered, trying not to imagine the pain he must have suffered in the demon's nest. *Enduring, indeed.* He opened his mouth to speak but Palarian placed a finger over his lips and shook his head. To endure must also mean to remain silent.

Down a webbed tunnel, past hideously large black spiders with brilliant red underbellies, they found a soft silver glow illuminating a room just around a bend. Talis and Palarian crept along slowly, mindful of luminescent worms that dropped from the ceiling in search of prey, their hungry mouths lined with needle-like teeth.

Then they found a room filled with silky-wet eggs, their black sheen reflecting the eerie silver light from pus-filled sacs clinging to the ceiling. Something terrible stirred from within the sacs. Silver iridescent bodies that radiated maliciousness, black wings that twitched when you thought they were at rest, and eyes, sensuous green eyes craving life, craving the whole world. They were beauty and horror at the same time.

Talis wanted to scream and run from the cave, hands blazing fire to burn this hell into ash, but the sorcerer fixed his hands to the sides of Talis's head and forced him to stare at a demon spawn.

"The creature wills itself to you," Palarian whispered into Talis's ear. "You are fortunate to be chosen so quickly by one as powerful as she."

Fortunate was not what Talis was feeling, cursed, doomed, beyond salvation, that was what he felt. But the longer he gazed into the demon's eyes the more he felt a kinship, an understand oozing from her snake-eyes. She spoke to him, inside his mind, words slippery as silk, words every man desires to hear. *You are powerful and wise, the world is open to your grasp, men will fall and kneel before your greatness, nothing is outside the realm of your control.*

Images burned in Talis's mind, of him defeating the Jiserians and the undead hordes, and the feeling of power from the black crystal surging through his body until he truly felt he could do anything. *There are men and there are gods. You are a god. Feel immortality and infinity flow through you.* Talis wanted to shout that it was a lie, to resist the seductive urgings of the demon's tongue, but he couldn't refute what she said. What Aurellia had said at the Temple of the Goddess Nacrea, after its destruction, before the old sorcerer leapt into the world's portal: *We are the gods, we who possess the power of the twin forces.*

The creature writhed and resisted her cocoon, as if longing to break free.

"See, she stirs...she desires you." Palarian's voice was unnaturally shrill and high-pitched. Talis glanced at the sorcerer's face and was horrified to find he had no mouth. Talis instinctively put a hand to his own lips and felt only smooth skin across the place where his mouth had once been. Instead of reacting in terror, curiosity filled his mind. Was this all an elaborate illusion?

When he looked down again, he realized his hands had shriveled and grown claws, and he'd sprouted wings, black wings the sheen of glass, scaled and sharp. He was changing. Only then did he understand that he was *inside* one of those eggs on the ground, and that the world appeared dark and smoky because he was gazing out through the egg's membrane.

From those fibers attached to his stomach he felt dark, sickening nutrients entering his body, bringing sustenance needed by the dark creature he was changing into. *There are worlds of light and worlds of darkness,* the demon purred. *Darkness fills the universe.*

He remembered the words of Master Viridian, *Light is illumination on our journey.* Did Talis battle against the darkness? Did he care? The Goddess Nacrea's glorious face glowed in his mind's eyes, her voice soft and pure, *With light and love, darkness gives shape to the universe.* The Goddess of the Sun, her last words to him, praising darkness? And she gave him a black crystal, channeling vast amounts of power. But it was destroyed now, Talis thought.

What was the thing that Rikar had to endure? Was this torture? It felt as natural as running full-speed across a wind-swept plain, heart thumping in his chest. He could feel the power, a deep well, surging through him, dark lines spread across the universe, connecting him to the source. But where was the source? He reached out and tried to grasp it, and only found himself floating in a shadow mist.

His eyes snapped open, a hard and reptilian movement. The egg felt entirely too cramped and he desired to break free. His neck jerked forward and his hard-boned nose smashed through the egg's wet membrane. He staggered through, waddling uneasily, legs feeling stiff and awkward. His wings arched out, ripping through what was left of the egg, flapping thick silver liquid across the cave's dark walls.

Palarian stepped back quickly, eyes flared in terror, mouth open, gaping at the creature Talis had become. When Talis realized the fear was aimed at him, something snapped inside and he changed back to his human form. He looked down at his arms, they were no longer claws, and his wings had vanished.

225

"What happened to me?" Talis said, staring into Palarian's eyes.

The sorcerer glanced around the room, and leaned in conspiratorially. "You took on dragon form...the first human I've ever seen able to do such a thing."

"Dragon form? But how?" The loudness of Talis's voice startled himself, and he locked eyes with the demon twitching inside her sac on the ceiling.

"This is the Chamber of Transformation, the place of sorrows and regrets. Where you resist the seductions of the demons and find your true self in the process. So strange...you didn't even bother to resist." Palarian flashed an odd smile. "I've never seen anything like it, you just gave into everything and went along with it."

"But why did I become a dragon?"

"Everyone changes into something...the egg was waiting for you to come...as was the demon. You chose each other. The dragon form was within you waiting to come out."

That sounded ridiculous. A dragon form waiting inside? And yet he'd felt and seen the transformation for himself. There wasn't a doubt about it, he'd become a black dragon. Unless this was all some kind of a nightmare.

"You don't believe me, you're suspicious of what you just experienced?" Palarian sighed, a wry expression crossing his face. "Well, you'll believe the next step in your training...learning how to transform back into dragon form."

"What? Why would I want to do that? It felt horrible being a dragon, like I wasn't even myself."

"You'll still retain your thoughts and bodily control, but the dragon's mind and instincts definitely will affect you. You know little about dragons so naturally it feels foreign to you. That will come later, once you possess first-hand the knowledge of dragons."

"But there are no dragons on our world, they only exist in ancient mythology."

"Oh, there are dragons there, hiding away far to the north, on the Isles of Tarasen. And there are many dragons on my home world, too. But there are none here on this bleak planet."

Palarian aimed his hands at Talis. "Now, let's continue your training...learning the shadow spell of transformation. You've learned shadow spells using Rune Magic, and I've taught you how to perform Shadow Blink...Shadow Transformation is somewhat similar.

"Close your eyes and feel those same energy cords extending out from your stomach. Good, that's good, but stretch them out farther...no, feel an imaginary hand yanking them out even farther... Yes, that's right!"

Talis could hear crackles of electricity burst out in front of him. Was it him or Palarian? He resisted the urge to open his eyes to see.

"Keep concentrating, don't let your mind wander with thoughts and questions... Breathe deeply and focus on extending your cords of energy out a hundred feet."

A flurry of pops and crackling rang out near his stomach, so loud it hurt his ears. He felt the sharp, needle-like sensation of electricity striking his mid-section.

"That's better, any more and you'll create a thunderstorm." Palarian chuckled. "A different shadow spell... For now, picture those cords of energy wrapping up and back and all around you, enveloping you in a warm cocoon, like how you felt inside the egg. Your inner sight will turn mottled, like staring through the egg's membrane.

"No! That's too far, you'll choke yourself to death. Relax, let yourself drift a bit. Settle in to the feeling of nesting, encased in the warm membrane...that's better."

Talis did feel like he was back inside the egg, nestled in the warm, silver liquid, even though he knew he was standing next to Palarian. Or was he?

"Stop thinking... I can hear your thoughts echo off these cave walls. Everything is amplified in here. If you're not careful, you'll turn your demon against you. The mind is a powerful amplifier, either it works for you or against you. Control your thoughts! That's better... Now your energy cords are your own membrane, wrapped together they make your own egg. Feel the heat *bake* yourself and the transformation will naturally come."

Then a wave of dry heat washed over Talis, like being on sand in the height of a hot desert day. Something snapped inside himself, and he experienced the same sensation of transformation as before: wings sprouted, hands and arms shriveling to claws, face expanding to a hard snout.

"It's happening," Talis said, but his voice had changed to a low, growl that echoed across the chamber.

"Yes, bravo, you've succeeded in transforming...and on the first try!" Palarian stared in amazement at the beast that Talis had become. "It's almost too easy for you...dangerous, I wonder. Like your body craves the dragon form."

The once vast chamber felt suddenly cramped, and Talis realized he'd grown by a substantial amount. Maybe three or four times his original size? He cast a hungry gaze at Palarian, feeling an unnatural urge to feast.

"Don't look at me like that," the sorcerer said, chuckling. "I'm not dinner. One of the things you'll have to deal with is handling your dragon-instinct urges. But now is not the time. Hurry up and change back into your human form."

But Talis didn't feel like changing back. A massive desire to stretch his wings and take flight washed over him. He tried to control it but found himself powerless. After all, he'd always wanted to fly by himself. He resented the fact that the wizards of the Order refused to teach him the spell of flight. So why should he resist now?

Palarian shook his head vigorously in disagreement. "No, no, you mustn't, not here in the Netherworld. There's far too much risk... Please, change back, just picture yourself as a human."

Talis ignored the sorcerer's words and flapped his wings, relishing in the wind currents he was creating inside the chamber. Despite Palarian waving his arms, trying to contain Talis, it was useless. Talis pulled in his wings, aimed his snout towards the tunnel leading outside, and scurried up towards the light.

"Come back!" Palarian shouted after him. Talis could hear the sorcerer's footfalls recede into the distance. Soon the tunnel opened up to the stark bone sky of the Netherworld and the strange, haggard trees, their weird leaves blowing listlessly in the wind.

Suppressing reason and ignoring caution, Talis arched out his wings full and stretched them wide, taking in the feeling of the wind racing up the rocks. He shook his head in delight and opened his jaw wide, feasting in the sensation of the air churning around inside.
Flight.

That was all he could think about. With one confident step he leapt off the rock ledge, flapped his wings, and fixed his eyes on the distant horizon.

24

Flight

Talis felt his stomach sink to his knees as he swooped down the rocky hillside, catching speed as he dove towards the banded-tree forest. His dragon instinct pushed him faster, flapping his great black, glassy wings in a mad rush, his snout snuffling against the gushing wind currents. He was free. Nothing about the alien landscape of the Netherworld seemed to bother him; there was wind, there was flight, he was free.

His dragon mind took over: to fly, to feast, to build a hoard. Some thoughts far in the distant recesses of his mind fought to be heard, but at the moment, those thoughts sounded like the tiny squeaks of a raving lunatic. The forest rushed past underneath, a wash of green and blood-red. Then he dove towards a field of golden grass, giant boulders littered amongst the expanse, nearing a long, snaking sea of emerald-green.

From what Talis sniffed in the air, flesh lurked below. His dragon jaws opened in anticipation and delight, eyes scanning the rocky landscape for movement. His stomach complained. Out of the corner of his eye he caught a glimpse of something moving slowly in a field of rocks. He stared at the place of movement and spotted an enormous rock-beast waddling along, camouflaged in the color and shape of a boulder. When Talis dove from the sky, in pursuit of the creature, the rock-beast froze so that it was nearly indiscernible from the rest of the boulders.

Talis landed in a great flapping of wings and scraping of claws against the rocky landscape. He could smell the blood pumping through the creature's body, and that made his own dragon blood pulse in a fury of expectation. But the rock-beast remained perfectly still, so Talis prodded the creature's hard, scaly side with his snout.

Still, no movement.

This time Talis opened his jaws, exposing his glistening, obsidian teeth, and scanned the creature's body for an opening to its soft flesh. But all the way around the creature was scaled down to the ground like a turtle retreated into its shell. A wild rage possessed him at the inability to find flesh to devour. He flapped his wings, raising himself up and slammed against the rock-beast. When the creature refused to move, he scraped his claws against the creature's scaly surface, finding purchase between a gap in the scales.

With a rush of wind and flapping wings he heaved the rock-beast up and over on its side. This time the creature bit the bait. The rock-beast slithered its long, snake-like neck out and around and snapped its jaws at Talis, but his dragon-reflexes were too fast for the creature. Talis kicked the beast and catapulted himself away from the rows of spiny teeth trying to sting him.

The rock-beast pushed itself up, six scaled and clawed legs digging into the ground, its spiny head swinging around, gazing at its attacker. When Talis shot himself forward, trying to sink his jaws into the beast's soft neck, the creature sent a black mist spiraling from its snout. The smell was rancid and acrid, like ruined eggs and vats of poison. Talis flapped his wings and hurled himself away from the poison, sneezed ten great explosions, his body trying to eject the toxic fumes.

But Talis could feel the poison working its way into his body. His blood pumped furiously, speeding the path to his death. He tried to control himself, control his dragon desires to fight and maim and devour the rock-beast now chattering its way towards him, a look of hunger in the creature's eyes. Prey turned predator.

He would die out here, even his dragon mind was surrendering to the crippling poison working its way towards his heart. In a mad rush, Talis seized his moment of weakness to gain clarity of thought. He would *not* die out here in the alien landscape of the Netherworld. The words of Palarian came rushing in, *Just picture yourself as a human. Do it now!*

So he did, and the agony of transformation felt worse than death, with the poison magnified in his now human body. He clenched his chest from the pain as the rock-beast mauled the ground in pursuit, the ground shaking, the beast's yellow eyes puzzled at his transformation. What was a meal was now only a morsel.

Talis knew he had to get away from here but the pain in his heart was so great he couldn't lift his hands to cast a spell. Then the lesson he'd recently learned from Palarian flashed in his mind's eye. He felt the energy fibers circling out wildly from his stomach, and remembered how to feel and find the shadow strands. He grabbed ahold of any he could find, desperate to escape. His eyes landed on distant, dreary mountains, and in a flash, he felt his stomach tugged as he blinked a vast distance away.

Thunder rumbled around him as the red rain poured down, soaking the ashen ground. Peals of lightning like the thousand fingers of the gods cascaded across the grey and bone horizon. The pain sunk deeper into his heart, so horrible that he clenched up his face, biting down on his jaws until his mouth felt numb.

He was dying. Alone and in a foreign wasteland. His mother and father and sister were probably captives of the Jiserians, his city fallen to their enemies. *Or maybe Viceroy Lei has made a pact with the devil,* Talis thought. No matter how he looked at it, he'd failed. Failed to help save his city, failed to help Mara, failed to even help himself.

A surge of terrific pain pulsated through his heart, and he screamed, the sound echoing across the rocks. He whimpered, sinking down to his knees, and curled up like a sleeping dog. One more attack like that and his heart would stop for good. For all his knowledge of magic, for all his power, when the time he'd needed saving the most, he was helpless to heal himself.

Out of the wind and storm and rain a whorl appeared in the sky, a whorl of silver and black. Where the silver light was tinged with hope, the black was stained with death. Light and darkness, the living and the dead. Talis feebly lifted his head, staring into the whorl as lightning condensed around the form; he expected tortured faces, expected death—here before him—to summon and guide him down the journey to the Underworld.

To his death.

But only one face appeared through the whorl, a face wrinkled and hideous from years of tampering with the dark arts, a face that stared with curiosity and cruelty at Talis's broken form.

"Despite all I've seen over the many thousand years of my miserable existence, nothing exceeds this pathetic sight." Aurellia stepped onto the swamped soil, twisting the long, curly hair sprouting from the mole on his nose.

Talis tightened his jaw as he pushed himself up to sitting position, determined not to give Aurellia a reason to mock him any further. He would face his enemy and stare death down, riding a wave of shadows to oblivion.

"How is it that I find you here, amidst the Hills of Carrion?" Aurellia bent closer and sniffed Talis. "And you're wounded, poisoned even! How very strange... How did you manage to escape from Palarian?"

A small cough escaped Talis's mouth, and he leaned over to suppress the pain that raged through his chest. He could only allow himself shallow breaths, otherwise the agony would be too much.

"Unable to talk? Well, I suppose I have no choice but to care for you…can't have you dying on me like this…would be foolish of me." Aurellia sighed morosely. "Although, why should I help you? You don't offer anything in return, do you?"

Once again the pain seethed through Talis's heart, this time worse than before, like long needles piercing his chest. He closed his eyes and scrunched up his face, thinking of Mara, thinking of his family, thinking of the Goddess Nacrea.

"Absolute loyalty is generally expected at moments like this…an oath binding one's soul to mine, a blood pact, eternal consecration to my will and my power. Or do you prefer dying? You do remember the Underworld, don't you?"

Talis grimaced as he stared at Aurellia, images of Zagros and his vast horde flashed before him, the Grim March, the endless dance of war and death.

"What do you want from me?" Talis muttered, refusing to lock eyes with the dark lord.

"Everything. I want freedom." Aurellia managed a small smile, an expression of hope flickering on his face for a second. "I want to return home. I've waited long enough. And you, young royal, can help me get what I want. I'd hoped you'd come sooner, but your loyalty to your city was stronger than your curiosity and love of adventure. So I commanded Rikar to lure you. When that didn't work, I summoned an old friend, Palarian, to join me on my return trip home."

"And he kidnapped Mara, forcing me here...."

"After the one you love." A coy expression crossed Aurellia's face. "I set everything up for you, I even supplied your friend with the Tandria Scroll. I had faith that you of all wizards could master the portal spell. And here you are!" Aurellia spread his crooked arms wide.

The pain in Talis's heart flared white-hot, and he clenched his eyes close, thinking, *Just let me die!* He didn't want to give in to Aurellia, he refused to think what life would be like swearing a blood-oath to this hideous sorcerer. And yet he knew Mara and Nikulo were still here, trapped on this world, they'd be prisoners of the dark lord for life. Naru would permanently fall to the Jiserians, and his family...enslaved or killed?

When he opened his eyes to stare at Aurellia, the world had changed. Instead of the grim, wet scene of the Netherworld, he was inside a massive subterranean cavern, kneeling in front of the guards of the Underworld. Izria and Ishtia. The hooded wight-like figures stood guard at the entrance to the world of the dead, golden glyphs blazing atop the square stone entrance. Talis's mouth hung open as the guardians' eyes stared in his direction.

The pain in his heart was gone. A sick feeling twisted his stomach. He was dead.

Talis felt a leathery hand on his shoulder. He spun around and glimpsed the pale eyes of Aurellia staring sadly at him.

"Your heart has stopped. You stand at the threshold of the Underworld. As a royal, upon your death, your parents have the sacred right to offer a blood sacrifice to Zagros, Lord of the Dead, and secure your place amidst the Fair Seas, free from torture, a life of eternal bliss." A wry smile wrinkled Aurellia's lips. "But alas, your parents have no idea you're dead. And I doubt Zagros would hear your plea in here, not after your last journey into the Underworld."

Morose laughter escaped Talis's mouth as he hung his head in disbelief. Not only would his friends and family suffer all their lives, but Aurellia made it clear that he'd suffer for eternity. *The Grim March, everlasting war and pain.* He had no choice but to swear an oath to Aurellia. But wasn't that what he wanted anyways? Ever since the Order of the Dawn had disintegrated after Master Viridian's death, he lacked a true master, one who could teach him both the ways of light and darkness. Aurellia was that master.

"Choose now," Palarian said, his voice somber. "The guardians of the Underworld are coming to steal your soul."

"I choose life." *I choose to make my own fate.* "I swear fealty to you." *Until I find a way to let death eat your soul and free me from my oath.*

A wide grin spread across Aurellia's face. "A wise decision. We must act quickly, else Izria and Ishtia devour your soul." He retrieved a curved, ornate dagger, rubies embedded on the hilt, and aimed it at Talis's hand. "A drop of royal blood and your life will be restored...forever. I am the immortal-maker, the time keeper, the assassin of the gods."

The tiny prick roared pain across Talis's body. The blood burst out, splashing his face, and he looked up, seeing the red rain of the Netherworld spilling from the lightning-etched clouds. He heard the whoosh of the churning shadow portal behind him, and glimpsed Aurellia's triumphant face as he dragged Talis back through the portal.

25

Unexpected Ally

Talis inhaled a huge gulp of air, relishing in the expulsion of pain from his chest. What had he done, swearing fealty to a monster? Waves of strange, hot currents coursed through his body. He felt completely changed…invincible even, and his body pulsed with power. He glanced around the dark cathedral cavern, silver and gold torches sending living shadows crawling across earthen walls. A long table draped in black silk held jars, clay tablets, scrolls, and leather-bound books.

Palarian stood at the head of the table, staring grimly at Talis. Aurellia flanked around at the opposite side, his long black robe dragging along an embroidered rug with illustrations of demons, heroes, and gods slaying lesser foes. He stopped at the head of the table, peering into a glass jar filled with luminous heads floating in a clear liquid.

"Our enemies fear what we'll do to them," Aurellia said, rotating the jar to inspect the various heads bobbing inside. "Now that you are one of us, they'll fear you as well."

He lifted his cold eyes to gaze at Talis. "Welcome to immortality." He raised the curved dagger he'd used to prick Talis's finger. "The Zacrane Dagger, bringer of immortality, usable only once each hundred thousand days. I've not used it in over a thousand years. As you can now understand, I don't grant this gift lightly."

Talis scowled, suspicious of why Aurellia would do this…what did he want from him?

"Why did I grant the gift to you? An arrogant young royal that despises me…don't deny it, I can see it in your eyes. You merely misunderstand me."

Palarian cleared his throat, and Talis swung his gaze to the other side of the table, where the old sorcerer had decided to sit on an ornately carved chair, sumptuous red silk padding the seat.

"He's just a boy, Aurellia. We knew he'd be like this, suspicious and angry. Rightfully so, I did kidnap his girl, he should feel malice."

"Yes, indeed, and perhaps that will only prove to make him stronger. I can mold him."

"You're getting old," Palarian said, aiming a scowl at Aurellia. "I believe it's time for youth and foolishness to reign, not to be molded by an old immortal's outdated notion of how things should work."

"Do you dare challenge me?" Aurellia raised an eyebrow at the old sorcerer. "He's sworn to me now, mine to command, mine to mold…he will be shaped in the old ways…."

"The old ways." Palarian scoffed. "Balance and focus, first the light then the darkness, steer the mind into emptiness. Hah! I've had it up to my throat in the old ways. What good has it done?"

Aurellia sneered at him. "Lecherous viper…you sting me with your words. The ancient plan I put forth with *my* elders—you included—thousands of years ago is finally playing itself out. We will return to Vellia, to our home, and claim what is rightfully ours."

"You made the mistake of leaving me on that miserable planet…after four thousand years you summon a World's Portal and fail to bring me along?"

"Foolish man, you left Darkov, you swore independence from the Dominion, you claimed the Tarasen Isles as your own."

"And when you needed me, when you realized you were stuck here, halfway to Vellia, only *then* did you summon me? Oh! Palarian, old friend, go to Naru in the Nalgoran Desert, and bring the boy to me. Well I did my part, I brought him here, and his friends, now you plan to mold him in the old ways… Look at me!"—Palarian thumped a hand on his chest—"I'm molded in the old ways. Isn't it pathetic? Look at what a miserable wretch I've become." Why was the old sorcerer defending him? Talis wondered.

Aurellia grinned devilishly. "At least you're still alive after all these years. But all that can quickly change." He pointed a finger at Palarian.

"I know all about your form of magic, and it doesn't frighten me. You fail to realize what a thousand years of independent study can bring to a sorcerer."

"Those years have been kind to me also." Aurellia sidled along the head of the table until he faced Palarian, with only the hideous rug between them.

Palarian shook his head, an amused expression on his face. "You live an indolent life, letting others fight your wars, searching for apprentices that might be *the one*. But your complacency will prove your downfall."

"Why are you so interested in protecting the boy? What did you see inside the Netherworld?"

"That was another mistake you made, sending me in there to train him." A devious look flashed across Palarian's eyes. "Wouldn't you like to know…."

"Oh, I'll find out, all right. I always do." An explosion of shadows and lightning burst out from Aurellia's fingertip, engulfing Palarian in a raging storm cloud. Talis felt the muscles around his skull clench because of all the electricity in the air. He stumbled, shrinking back to the earthen walls.

Talis stared at the storm, trying to see what had happened to the old sorcerer.

"That's ineffective against me now," Palarian said, his voice coming from a dark mass behind where Aurellia stood.

The dark lord whirled around to face Palarian, snapped out his hands, and cords of golden light curled out from the ground beneath Palarian, swirling and searching, trying to ensnare. The cords sucked in the black mass, draining the protection around Palarian. Aurellia commanded the golden cords to wrap around the old sorcerer's legs, burning flesh and sending off a cloud of smoke.

Palarian shrieked in pain, jetting out cords of his own from his fingertips, allowing them to wrap around Aurellia's neck. The cords strangled the dark lord, causing his face to bulge, red and angry, his hands trying to tear them away. Talis was surprised to see Aurellia struggling against the force of Palarian's power.

Aurellia shot out a burst of black light, causing all the cords in the vicinity to melt into ash. The two sorcerers glowered at each other, puzzled and flushed, as if wondering what to do next.

"I told you, I've had a thousand years of study to beat you." Palarian's eyes flashed with haughtiness.

Aurellia wiped beads of sweat from his brow. "I am surprised by how you've grown in power and skill...perhaps the distance and ruggedness of Tarasen has made you stronger. But your mind is still weak...the pain of the memory of your father's death still plagues you." He raised a hand to his temple.

Palarian howled like an old wolf, fleeing to his knees, writhing with his hands clenched over his skull. "You think you can beat me using mind tricks? I've hardened myself through years of solitude and torture. You cannot hope to break through...the pain of loss has left me."

"Then I'll have to kill you outright." Aurellia aimed his fingers at the old man, and everything in the room seemed to blink and shake quickly left and right. Palarian's face was frozen in an angry scowl, body rigid and locked in an attempt to raise his hands. Talis found that he himself was unable to move, but somehow his eyes could see everything in the room, including his curled up figure and the wall behind. He had the eerie sensation of being jetted outside of his body, forced to play witness to the hideous scene.

A quavering wall of electric shadow mesh ejected out of Aurellia's hands and wrapped around Palarian like an octopus choking prey. The mesh flashed silver light, and hundreds of twisted lines of black currents pulsed with a sickening slowness. The color and life was slowly being drained from Palarian's face and his upraised hands.

Talis refused the idea of the old sorcerer dying. He had tried to protect him, and despite being forced to kidnap Mara and lead him into this trap, he sensed the old man had a good heart. So he allowed his anger to rage inside, until it was brimming over inside, the heat and the fire breaking out of the cage that had trapped him.

Aurellia's eyes glanced nervously at Talis, shifting his focus for one crucial moment, allowing Palarian to strike back with several shadow creatures flying out of his hands and attaching themselves to Aurellia's figure, gleaming fangs, spurts of blood and ash, growls of fury. Aurellia swung a bloodied arm around, a dark creature gnawing on his elbow, and sent an invisible shockwave howling at

Palarian, knocking him twenty feet back against the earthen wall.

When Aurellia was about to raise his hands and fight the shadow creatures eating at his body, Talis listened to his anger, drawing in a vast amount of power from the crystal, and shot out a burst of Light Magic at the dark lord. The light was so strong it illuminated the room in a blinding flash that lingered for an unbearable span of time. Soon the light faded, and Talis's eyes slowly adjusted to the darkness of the subterranean chamber.

Aurellia had vanished.

26

The Crystal

Talis pushed himself to his feet, feeling empty and sore from the powerful outburst of magic. Off in the corner of the room, Palarian stirred, shaking his arms and head like he'd drunk too much wine. He glanced around, a puzzled look on his face.

"Where did he go?" Suspicion flashed in Palarian's eyes. "Did you see him open a shadow portal or somehow escape?"

"I attacked him with Light Magic while he was focused on you."

"So that's where the burst of light came from...I shielded myself from light the moment I sensed the power rising." Palarian stumbled over to where Talis stood, sizing him up like he'd done something terribly wrong. "Did you actually kill him?"

Talis shook his head, unsure exactly what had happened. "One moment there was an enormous ball of light, and the next moment he was gone."

Palarian frowned, and slumped back on a chair by the table. "Aurellia...dead?" He mumbled incoherent words, lost in world of his own.

"Are you alright? You were trying to kill each other...I only tried to help."

"How could he be dead? Not by a burst of light from a young whelp...." The old sorcerer lifted his head suddenly, sniffing the air, then settled his gaze on Talis. "Well, whatever it is you've done has given us a moment of opportunity, a way of possible escape. Let's not waste another moment."

"But where will we go?" Talis furrowed his brow, uncertain of how to proceed. "And what about my friends?"

Palarian waved away his concerns. "They're safe...but none of us will remain alive if we stay here much longer. If his loyal Elders find out what you've done, if they realize their Master is gone...then watch out."

The old sorcerer flung his hands forward and a silver portal appeared. He grabbed Talis's wrist, and pulled him inside. They immediately entered a vast stone room, sunlight streaming in through far windows, with Mara and Nikulo and Charna off in the corner, and a minder dressed in black robes stood scowling at the head of a long, wooden table.

With a flick of his finger, Palarian sent fibrous strands over the minder, engulfing him in a sticky web. The man appeared confused, then dazed, and finally fell asleep.

"Talis!" Mara squealed, racing over to him. Tears spilled from her eyes as she hugged him, and at this moment, nothing ever had ever felt so good.

"We were so worried about you," she murmured in his ear. "They refused to tell us a thing. We've been waiting here for weeks."

"Weeks?" Talis said, shocked it had been so long. "But it only seemed like a day...inside the Netherworld." He glanced over at Nikulo ambling over towards them, a grin played nicely on his face. "You're looking healthy...did Aurellia cure you of the poison?"

Nikulo's face clouded suddenly, as if remembering a painful memory. "He did, for certain promises... I had no choice."

"Like swearing allegiance to him?" Talis studied Nikulo, and sat next to him. He told Nikulo and Mara the story of what had happened inside the Netherworld, of his transformation into a dragon, and misadventure leading him to be cured by Aurellia. When he got to the part of the battle between Aurellia and Palarian, Nikulo's mouth flopped open, and he snuck a glance at the old sorcerer standing by one of the windows, staring out over the horizon.

"So our vow to him is broken?" Nikulo said. "Because Aurellia is dead?"

Talis shrugged, wrinkling his nose at the hint of sulfur in the air. "We've got to get out of here...find our way back home."

"And that means finding a powerful enough crystal to open a portal back to our world?" Mara crossed her legs and leaned forward in her overstuffed chair.

"If it's the last thing I do, I'll find a way to bring us back to Naru." Talis touched two fingers to his forehead, sanctifying the ancient vow.

"What if there's not a home waiting for us when we return?" Mara whispered, her voice soft and tinged with sadness.

"I can't believe that's the case. Between Mistress Cavares, Master Jai, Master Grimelore, and my father, I believe we can rebuild the life we once knew."

"But my father is a traitor, Talis... It's unthinkable to me, but how can I disbelieve it? I love him, he's my father, but how can I go back and face him? I'm so ashamed of belonging to House Lei."

Talis shook his head, refusing to accept any association of Mara to her father. "You're not your father, and the Lei family name is more than one man...you can change that, if you want. Think of your history. House Storm and House Lei were allies together over hundreds of years. Don't let your father ruin the Lei family reputation."

"And you'll help me change all that?" Mara leaned forward and held Talis's hand. He felt a warm fire swirl inside his stomach.

"Of course I will...I'll do anything for you."

Nikulo chuckled softly, and pushed himself up from his chair, causing Talis and Mara to shift their gaze towards him. "I know this is all very touching, and I don't mean to get in the way of young love, but…."

Talis felt his face flush, and sneaking a quick glance at Mara caused him to realize her face was red with embarrassment. She averted her eyes after she noticed him looking.

"Pray tell," Nikulo said, "how are we going to get back home?"

"I know the way back…." Palarian kept his gaze fixed out the window. "If we have a sufficiently strong crystal, we can open a world's portal."

Nikulo frowned. "Why would you help us go back home? You're the one who kidnapped Mara in the first place, and tricked us into coming here. Didn't you do it all to return to your own planet?"

"Would you believe me if I said I wanted to make amends for all my misdeeds?" Palarian stared at Nikulo, deep wrinkles on his forehead bunched together.

"No, I wouldn't." Nikulo made a ridiculous expression like nothing could make him believe the old sorcerer. "You're just trying to trick us into getting the crystal for you."

"Do you have any other choice? I know the runes to the forty-eight planets in the known universe. How many do you know?" The old sorcerer coughed slightly. "Oh, let's see now…exactly one. And you happen to be on that planet. Silly of you, really…."

"But how do you know there are even suitable crystals on this planet?" Mara twisted up her mouth, as if displeased with the idea.

"My teachers from ancient days—long ago when I was young and naive like you—taught us that this planet was one of the binding planets, rich with hidden crystals needed to port between worlds. Believe it or not, the place you ported into this planet was home to an ancient temple, with a powerful crystal underneath. When those of our planet— from Vellia—banished us to your planet, they destroyed that temple and the crystal."

Palarian pointed at Talis's backpack. "Shall we hunt for crystals?"

"Well, you did help fight against Aurellia...." Talis still didn't trust the old sorcerer, but he was right, he didn't have any choice. Even if he could locate a crystal, it wouldn't do him any good.

So he swung around his backpack, and retrieved the Surineda Map. "But you have to promise to help us get home. And not only do you have to show us the rune symbol for our planet, you have to show us the symbol for Vellia."

"Do you want to go and visit someday?" Palarian raised an eyebrow. "We have vast hordes of dragons on Vellia. But I suspect it would be far too dangerous for you, unless you learned how to better protect yourself."

"I simply want to understand the difference between the runes...so you can't trick us."

Palarian chuckled. "I could still trick you, since you'd have to believe my word that this rune represents this planet. Besides, if we find a powerful enough crystal, you should be able to go to your planet, and I should be able to open a portal to Vellia. Simple, right?"

If they could find such a crystal. But Talis remembered the shattering of the old crystal at the first Temple of the Sun, when Aurellia had summoned a world's portal, and thought that most crystals could probably only sustain one spell. The amount of power channeled through the crystal was too great.

Talis unravelled the Surineda Map, feeling the heat rush into his arms and down his spine. He glanced at Mara and Nikulo, and they nodded back in support. Palarian held an eager, hungry look in his eyes that made Talis feel really nervous about using the map to find crystals. But he told himself he had no choice. This was their only way back home.

In his mind he commanded the map to display a view of the world wide enough to cover the land they'd traveled, and he held the feeling and image of the black crystal, given to him by the Goddess Nacrea. The crystal had a peculiar quality about it, surging and strong, and subtle and soft at the same time. When the picture was clear, he opened his eyes and studied the map.

Nothing. The map displayed no points of light, and no crystals.

"How can that be?" Talis muttered.

Mara shuffled up alongside him, and peered over his shoulder. "Try getting a wider view of the world."

So Talis closed his eyes again, and imagined zooming the map's view out twice as far from what it showed, and kept his desire to see crystals firmly in his mind. Far to the south, away from where they'd travelled west to east, a sea appeared along the coastline.

"An ocean!" Mara said, tapping the map.

Palarian grimaced. "The Grey Sea...a very nasty place...far unlike the beautiful oceans of your world. On this world the seas are quite inhospitable to human life."

"Still nothing," Talis said. "I'm going to expand the map out even farther."

Soon the map showed more of the Grey Sea until a golden light pulsed amidst the sea far to the south.

"Bless the Goddess Shade, and her tricks she performs on the world." Palarian frowned, and rubbed his scraggly chin. "The crystal is inside the Grey Sea...."

27

The Grey Sea

Even after searching different parts of the world using the Surineda Map, shifting and zooming in and out, Talis still couldn't find another crystal.

"There have to be more crystals," Palarian muttered. "This world is seeded with them. How are you commanding the map to find the crystals?"

"I'm remembering the black crystal, and its feeling."

The old sorcerer snapped his fingers, his eyes lightning up. "That's the problem! There are many other kinds of suitable crystals. You've just not had enough experience with the various other types of crystals. If I had, you could establish a firm image and feeling, and search for them."

"Well, then we wouldn't need to search for them." Nikulo gave Palarian a bland expression.

"We've found a crystal, why can't we try and get it?" Talis glanced at the old sorcerer.

"There are a thousand reasons why you'd never even think about entering the Grey Sea. Ravenous sea monsters the size of this castle, swarms of poisonous jellyfish, sea snakes the length of Naru's wall... And you still want to go?"

Nikulo shrugged. "Sure, why not? I need more poison to add to my collection."

An exasperated expression flashed across Palarian's face. "And how do you propose even going underneath the Grey Sea?"

"Listen," Nikulo whispered, "we entered the Underworld and met Zagros, Lord of the Dead. Have you been to the Underworld? I didn't think so. How hard could this Grey Sea be compared to that?"

"Much harder, you fat little whelp." Palarian scowled at Nikulo. "You think this is all so easy? How can you be so cavalier about life and death. Your friend here almost *died* inside the Netherworld."

"What makes you think the crystal is *underneath* the Grey Sea? Perhaps there's an island there, or something else." Talis scanned their eyes for a hint of understanding.

Palarian and Nikulo both breathed heavily in frustration, but they kept quiet, staring at Talis as if his idea might be valid.

"The only way to find out is to look closer at the crystal," Mara said, and scooted up next to Talis.

Talis closed his eyes again, and asked the map to move closer to the crystal, displaying any islands or anything surrounding the crystal. When he opened his eyes he gasped. The crystal was moving slowly amidst the ocean.

"How is that possible?" Mara said, peering in closer to inspect the map.

"What? Let me see...." Nikulo waddled over to the map, and grunted in surprise. "The crystal is floating on the sea?"

Palarian snorted, and Talis turned his gaze from the map, wondering why the old sorcerer had such a humorous expression on his face. "I'm guessing the crystal is lodged within a giant sea creature. Try your map, command it to show any larger creatures."

So Talis did what the sorcerer suggested, and to his amazement, the map showed a large dot amongst many other dots.

"There, exactly as I suggested." Palarian looked up at Nikulo. "How good are you at controlling the mind's of creatures?"

Nikulo chuckled. "I'm good at poisoning them to death."

"I doubt that will work," Palarian said, his expression dripping in sarcasm. "But seriously, can you control beasts?"

"I can try, but no guarantees. The human mind is very different than the mind of creatures."

"How are we even supposed to get out there?" Mara said.

"Leave that to me," Palarian said, gesturing towards the open window. "I know how to fly."

With one smooth gliding motion, the sorcerer swept through the window and floated in the air, gesturing them closer. He snapped a finger at Talis, then Charna, and the poor lynx yowled and hissed as she started rising into the air.

"It's okay, girl," Talis said, holding Charna in his arms. He jumped out of the window, and relished in the feeling of weightlessness that came with flight.

"Do we have to fly?" Nikulo muttered, staring uneasily down the steep drop outside the window.

"Feel free to stay...the minder will be waking up soon enough."

"On second thought, let's get out of here." Nikulo motioned for Palarian to cast the spell, and closed his eyes as he flew out of the castle.

Mara followed them out, giggling and flapping her arms like a bird. "This is just like flying in dreams!"

"But unlike in dreams, when you fall you don't wake up...you splat on the ground." Nikulo's face twisted up at the thought.

"Enough already," Palarian said, frowning. "To move just think where you want to go in your mind."

The sorcerer raised his eyes towards the clouds and sped off, Talis and Mara and Nikulo chasing after him. The higher they went, Talis thought they would freeze, but realized they were protected by some kind of bubble that kept the cold and wind out. The ground fell away below them as they rose up over the clouds, then out across the puffy landscape, reminding Talis of walking through mist and fog.

They crossed the jagged mountains, pinnacles stabbing up through the clouds, until they swept down over a vast, barren plain that edged the Grey Sea. A wall of black fog hung over the ocean, like a pack of wild dogs feasting on prey.

Before they entered the bleak mass, Palarian paused, hovering in the air, waiting for Talis to come close.

"The map should guide us through that mess... We need to avoid the fog itself as much as possible, ghosts and wights and such. We'll fly along the surface of the sea, mindful of creatures breaching the surface for a tasty bite of human flesh."

Talis grimaced at the idea of what lay in store for them down there. He flew over to Nikulo, and handed him Charna, who seemed terrified at the idea of leaving Talis's arms. As Talis unfurled the Surineda Map, he realized the sorcerer had guided them well this far; directly south lay the crystal, the beast moving slowing through the sea.

Only the fog and the dangers of the Grey Sea lay between them and the crystal. As Talis and the others swept down towards the mottled coast, jets of electrified water shot up from holes dotting the rocky beach. Talis veered away from the scintillating streams, and wondered what kind of creature lived within the holes.

Soon they soared over the pounding waves, whitecaps and sea foam swirling amidst the dark murk of the sea.

Massive shapes tunneled under the surface, sending a prickling sensation along his back. Palarian led the group up above the water until fog fingerlings brushed them as they flew, causing an avalanche of screaming voices to ravage Talis's mind.

Talis instinctively dove away from the fog, trying to ignore the ghostly forms floating along, their eyes gaping holes of blackness. But when he edged closer to the water, a green, scaled head shot out, jaws the size of a castle, the creature's long neck twisting around, pale eyes guiding towards them.

"Be careful," Palarian shouted, and Talis lurched up in response. "Let's pray to the gods that the fog doesn't descend."

Nikulo scowled at the old sorcerer. "What do we do if the fog *does* come down? I can't imagine how we'll fight those sea creatures and whatever nasty things are up there in the fog."

"Think of it as an opportunity—" Palarian stopped flying and squinted ahead. "An opportunity you will likely have rather soon."

Farther ahead the space between the ocean and the black fog narrowed to a sliver. Talis felt his heart sink, wondering how they were going to get through. There was only the smallest chance they could slip through unnoticed by the sea creatures below. But as Palarian sped ahead, seemingly determined to break through anyways, hundreds of dark shapes wriggled beneath the surface, tracking their flight.

"They're following us!" Mara yelled, soaring up alongside Talis. "We're never going to get through."

The closer they got to the surface (as the fog kept pressing lower), the more the army of sea creatures writhed and twisted about, breaking through the surface, flipping around in a fury of expectation. Some of the creatures were impatient, choosing instead to attack others close by, painting red washes in the Grey Sea. And this seemed to only whip up the crowd below into a feeding frenzy. More creatures joined in the attack, biting and tearing and bashing smaller creatures.

"Now's your opportunity to practice," Palarian said, eying Nikulo. "One of the larger beasts."

Nikulo framed his hands around his face, peering into the ocean. He nodded, apparently satisfied at an enormous creature gliding serenely through the bloodied waters. Soon the giant beast raised its snake-like head above the surface, black eyes peering around as if wondering who was intruding on its thoughts. Nikulo's hands were clenched over his temples, face contorted as he fought the creature's mind.

"Don't fight it...seduce it with pleasant thoughts. Win the creature over as your friend," Palarian said. "You can't turn such a beast into a zombie, however you can influence its actions."

At the sorcerer's words, Nikulo's face softened a bit, he inhaled, cleared his throat, and tried again. This time the sea creature shook its head, sending a shower of water beads cascading across the sky. Its eyes seemed more focused now, and it looked around at the other smaller beasts, as if suddenly realizing it was hungry.

"There!" Palarian shouted. "You've done it, look, the beast is feeding... Have it move along with us as we fly, the others will be distracted."

Nikulo's concentration was so complete that Talis and Mara had to pull him along, each holding an arm. As they flew along, tracking the massive sea creature's path, the other smaller beasts darted out of the way, leaping out of the sea, trying to avoid the enormous snapping jaws of the creature Nikulo controlled.

But the horde of angry sea beasts around the giant seemed to discover it was better to coordinate their attacks, and they swarmed around, biting chunks of blubber off the monster. Talis and the others had reached a narrow point where the fog nearly reached the sea. With the sea creatures distracted, they swooped down and sped through the gap between fog and sea, brushing sea foam as it splashed up into the air.

"We made it!" Mara said, and they flew up and away from the crashing waves as the fog rose on the other side. The vast expanse of the Grey Sea opened up, and even stray bits of sun managed to sneak through breaks in the black fog. Talis glanced down at the Surineda Map, and realized the sea creature and the crystal had stopped moving. He commanded the map to move in closer to the crystal, and Talis discovered it was now, for some reason, lodged on an island not too far in the distance.

"Over there...an island." Talis pointed towards a spot of green and glittering light far off in the distance.

Mara and Palarian swooped over to peer at the map. Mara held her breath.

"What kind of a sea creature goes on an island?"

"We'll find out soon enough." Talis raced off, chasing the golden light shimmering off the island.

When the island was close enough for Talis to recognize a white, glittering beach and palm trees swaying in the soft breeze, he felt his shoulders sag in relaxation, hoping they were finally past the dangers of the Grey Sea. But whatever creature that had thrived in the sea was now somewhere on land, roaming the island.

Nearer to the shore Talis could see hundreds of black shapes littering the beach, writhing about like an insect swarm. When they arrived, hovering over the beach, Talis recognized the shapes as small black crabs, darting around, chasing an afternoon snack.

"Now I'm getting hungry." Nikulo slapped his belly. "Do you suppose they'll roast up nicely?"

"Really? You just ate a few hours ago," Mara said.

"That was half-a-world away... We've done much adventuring since then." Nikulo grinned and descended to the beach, and the sand crabs scurried away like mice.

"I don't suppose a little barbecue would do us any harm." Palarian glanced around the beach. "How far away is the crystal?"

Talis studied the Surineda Map still in his hands, commanded it to move in closer, and saw that the crystal was farther ahead inside the palm tree forest.

"Not far at all... We might as well have something to eat." Talis put the map away, and aimed his fingers at the crabs.

"Wait...let me have the honors of catching our dinner." Nikulo chuckled to himself, raised his hands to his temples, and focused on the scuttling crabs. Soon the creatures bumped around, confused, and eventually lined up to proceed along an odd march towards them.

"Look...the march of the black crabs," Mara said, and giggled at the crabs bobbing back and forth on their dazed charge towards them. Talis grabbed a few driftwood pieces scattered along the shore, and assembled a bonfire, quickly sending flames to hiss away at the water locked inside. The flames crackled and found purchase amongst the now dry wood, issuing the stench of burning seaweed still entangled on the logs.

"My contribution," said Palarian, summoning an iron cauldron and iron tripod to hold it above the fire. The flames licked the coarse bottom of the pot, spreading water vapors dancing along its surface. Inside the sorcerer had summoned saffron-smelling soup filled with tomatoes, potatoes, onions, and dotted with red peppers.

"Go fetch some clams…there, along the rocks, I think you'll find some if you look. Crabs and clams, now if we only had shrimp." The old sorcerer licked his lips as he stirred the stew with a summoned wooden ladle.

Talis and Mara raced off for the sea, dancing over cringing crabs, musing over shimmering sea shells the size of Nikulo's head, splashing water into glittering beads that flew from their feet. From danger and black skies to a warm blue horizon and an emerald sea, Talis inhaled fresh air tinged with salt, and searched for clams amidst the rocks and foamy water.

Mara's delicate hand sliced into the sea, and squealing, she raised a fat clam as if holding a trophy. Her face pronounced that she was the winner, having found the prize first, her eyes taunting Talis, daring him to do better. He grunted, deciding instead to splash her with a heavy load of water, her face shocked and thrilled at the coldness.

"You didn't just do that!" She kicked an arcing stream into his face, the salt stinging, bitter and sweet on his lips. A grin spread over his face as the water dripped down, and he lunged forward and grasped her, determined to dunk her completely. She twisted and spun around, not really trying to break free; his grip held and he launched them both to the side, and a wave crashed into them.

She was close now, so close he could almost hear her eyelashes blinking furiously against the salt sting. Had he only now just noticed her lips, drenched in the sea, laughing mysteriously, her eyes glittering with mischief?

Instead of pushing him away, she sank back, still holding onto his wet clothes, until they drifted in the water. She stared at him, glancing down occasionally at the crystal sea, but always brought her gaze back up to his, her breath quick.

Talis could feel his heart jumping in his chest; his mouth felt suddenly dry.

"Thank you...Talis...for coming for me." She blinked, sending drops of water fluttering. "I don't think anyone else but you would've done that."

He shrugged, blushing, feeling warm despite the cold water. "Er...it was nothing. You would've done the same thing if it was me. We have to take care of each other. We're a team."

"We are?" Mara's smile spread across her face, cheeks red and flushed. "Yes, we are, aren't we. I hope so...I mean I always hoped so, since we were little. You know what I mean?"

Talis didn't know what she meant, but he smiled back, and nodded his head. Was she talking about something more than just friendship? When she moved closer, her eyes looked down, fingers inspecting a loose button on his shirt.

"I want to stay like this...so perfect...why can't it always be like this? No fights between kingdoms or our families...just you and me, the sun and the waves and the blue sky going on forever. I don't want it to ever end."

"It'll be alright, I promise." Talis lifted Mara's chin and gave her a warm, reassuring smile. "When we get home we can make things right...together...I'm sure of it."

"You mean it?"

Talis nodded, staring into her eyes, until her face glowed with affection. He motioned his head towards the beach. "Find a few more clams? You seem to have a knack for it."

She pushed him away and grinned devilishly. "You're just jealous...I'm a better hunter than you." As if to prove her point, she dove into the water, and retrieved two more clams the size of fists. After they'd collected all they could carry, they trudged up the beach, beaming at Nikulo and Palarian.

"Ho, ho! Quite a load," the old sorcerer said, and plopped the clams into the bubbling stew.

"You sure took your time finding them...or maybe something else was occupying your minds." Nikulo grunted, raising an eyebrow at Talis and Mara.

"To be young again..." A fine smile crossed over the old man's face, and it seemed fond memories washed over him like a warm dew. "But to return home and visit the land of my youth, that would be my ultimate joy."

Nikulo frowned at Palarian. "You are taking us back home? I'm sure the idea of home is brimming with goodness to you, but we really need to get to *our* home, to Naru...not your planet, whatever you call it."

"Vellia...my world is called Vellia." The old sorcerer sighed as he stirred the stew, and shook his head as if nothing made sense anymore. "Why do I even bother? I follow Aurellia out here to this world on vain hopes of returning home. Is it wrong to wish such a thing? We share the same desire."

"Perhaps there is a way..." Talis tasted a bit of the stew and smiled. "What if we opened two portals at the same time?"

"What do you mean?" Mara said, edging her way along his side.

Talis glanced at Palarian, who wrinkled up his forehead, obviously considering the idea. "I mean if we shape two runes and cast the bindings at the same time, each of us summoning the power from the crystal at once, perhaps it will work. We can go to our world and you to yours...."

"That just might work...assuming the twin spells aren't too powerful to shatter the crystal. But all we need is enough power to open the portals...it might hold shape long enough to see us through."

"First we eat," Nikulo said, and opened his mouth expectantly. "Then you can test your theories all you want."

Palarian summoned a silver bowl with a flourish of his wrist, and scooped a generous portion of steaming crabs and clams and stew. Nikulo eagerly took the bowl, and nodded graciously as the sorcerer handed him a summoned silver spoon.

"Now dis is dewicious," Nikulo mumbled, bits of stew spilling from his mouth.

"Might help if you keep your mouth closed when you talk." Mara poked Nikulo in the ribs. "Is it really possible to summon two portals at once?"

Talis and Nikulo turned and stared at Palarian, who bobbed his head thoughtfully in response.

"It is theoretically possible... We'll both be drawing from the same power source. That's the problem and solution at the same time."

"Why is it a problem?" Mara accepted a bowl of stew from the old sorcerer.

Palarian's face darkened, and his eyes turned a pale grey. "If we fail to balance the twin portals, the power flowing through us will rip us apart... We'll die...instantly."

28

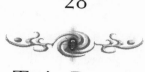

Twin Portals

Talis found that he was suddenly not hungry anymore. He cast a suspicious glance at the old sorcerer, and wished he hadn't suggested the possibility of opening twin portals. Mara stared up at Talis, her eyes dark and searching as if hoping he had an answer.

Nikulo broke the silence with a loud belch, and thumped his chest as a way of making an apology. "Wait…let me get this straight. Each of you open a portal, and each of you will be drawing power from the crystal at the same time, correct?"

Palarian nodded somberly. "One crystal and one power source."

"And the balancing part?"

"World portals require a tremendous amount of energy…when they are forming, they draw impossible spikes of energy that often crack or shatter the crystals trying to channel the power. Two portals at once…to different worlds…spikes in energy may occur at different times. It could lead to disaster. We'd have to balance, try to balance, anyways."

"And if we just opened one portal to our world, and you could open another one to yours?" Mara looked hopefully at the old sorcerer.

"The crystal may very well crack, and I'd be stuck here without another crystal of sufficient strength." Palarian motioned to Talis. "Your idea is valid, and it's been done before…by other sorcerers of legend, older than my time."

Talis coughed at the idea, unable to fathom a history that went back that long. "So we have no choice but to try it?"

"When you're faced with the impossible, face it, conquer it, don't give up until you've dreamed your world and made it into what you've always desired it to be. That's what a thousand years of solitude and tinkering with the dark arts has gained me: wisdom. Whatever you struggle for is always worth it in the end."

"We have a world we want to create." Talis gazed warmly at Mara, and she blushed in response. "We just need to return home."

Palarian cast his eyes towards the palm forest. "Shall we then?"

Talis unrolled the Surineda Map and frowned. "The crystal is moving farther inland…this way." He gathered his backpack and led the way up the beach towards the palms, their branches dancing under a stiff breeze that had started from the north. Charna dashed ahead through grassy undergrowth filled with fallen coconuts and shrubs and the occasional snake slithering out of sight.

They found a clearing with a stream and a wide path that had been trampled by something incredibly large. The stream was laced with flowers, bottle brush and orchids and gingers. Many trees along the way up the mountainside had been knocked aside. Talis discovered a massive clawed print twice the size of person.

"I'd hate to be stepped on by whatever beast made that print," Nikulo said, peering down into the hole left by the print.

"It's moving up in those mountains faster than we're walking." Talis pointed at the map.

Palarian cleared his throat and snapped a finger at Talis, and he experienced the weightless sensation of flying. He whistled to Charna, who bounded back towards him, and hissed in reaction to seeing them floating again.

"Come on, girl, I know you don't like flying, but I'll hold you and won't let go."

The lynx hesitated, her gold eyes staring at Talis, and finally she leapt into his arms, her paws wrapped around his neck. Soon they were up flying above the landscape, following the trodden path of the enormous creature. They kept lower to the ground, tracing the line of the stream as it jutted up over a hill that led to a broad pool and a waterfall. There were many massive prints along the pool's edge.

"The creature must have stopped to take a drink here…he was probably sick of drinking salt water."

Talis followed the trampled path around and up the next hill, through another forest until it reached a rocky cliff where the water came out of a bubbling spring. The cliff was several hundred feet high, and the creature's path led to the left where the way turned into grassland and eventually went down the hillside, back to another beach with clumps of sea grass scattered here and there. An enormous curved boulder sat in the middle of the beach.

"What's that? Is that a rock?" Mara said.

"That's no rock...look it's moving. I think we've found our sea creature." Talis dove towards the beast, and as he got closer, recognized the bumpy grey and brown shell, sharp ridged beak, and giant claws as belonging to a massive sea turtle. The turtle's claws dug into the sandy soil as if it was searching or preparing the ground for something.

Then the turtle turned to face them and Talis nearly fell from the sky.

"Its eyes!" Mara shouted. "They're black crystals...."

A deep rumbling came from the beast and smoke flared from its nostrils. The black faceted crystal eyes glowed with a piercing silver light. The turtle took slow thundering steps that caused the ground to shake. Talis flew over and peered into the hole that the creature was digging, and noticed a pile of dull white eggs.

As if reacting to a threat against its eggs, the turtle sent sparks of lightning from its eyes, igniting a surge of heat and pain throughout Talis's body. The force was so strong it slapped him from the sky and sent him and Charna tumbling over the sand and into a mass of seagrass. Charna hissed and scampered away, her hair standing up. Talis grasped his left shoulder as a dullness spreading down his arm, his heart pounding, and his chest felt like someone was pressing hard against it.

Out of the corner of his eye Talis could see Nikulo trying to control the beast, but the turtle just bellowed madly, swung its head around and gazed at his friend. Beams of dark light sliced through the air and struck Nikulo, causing him to stumble about as if drunk and dizzy, and he fell backwards onto the sand.

When Palarian clapped his hands, black strings snaked out and wrapped around the turtle, enveloping the beast in their entangling snare. Mara used the opportunity to race across the beach towards Talis.

"Are you alright?" she said, and helped him to his feet. His chest still felt numb and his legs were wobbly and weak.

"It was just trying to protect its eggs...over there in the hole...so many turtle eggs."

A smile spread over Mara's face. "Mama turtle...looks like Palarian has her settled down...she's sleepy now."

Talis sauntered over to where Palarian was tying the shadow cords to an iron rod lodged deep in the sandy soil. The sorcerer held an amused look on his face.

"Such an amazing mystical beast...imagine, crystals of such quality lodged in its eyes!" Palarian wagged his head from side to side.

"Will it hurt her if we cast the World's Portal spell?" Mara said, her eyes staring sadly at the turtle.

"I don't believe it will…painless, I would think…take a bit of her bite away from her, but that might not be a bad thing. But why are her eyes crystals…living crystals? Who formed her, or should I say which god made her?"

"Does it make it easier casting twin portals with two crystals?" Talis said.

Palarian frowned as if lost in thought. "Twin crystals…twin portals. I don't like the smell of it. Reminds me of a story I once heard in my youth, many thousands of years ago. But that couldn't happen, could it?"

What was he talking about? Talis thought. The old sorcerer started muttering to himself again, staring off at the black and grey fog wall far in the distance.

"But that would mean… no, not that. Not again…the ancients prevented that from ever happening again. Or are we at the beginning of another Kyrian Cycle?" The sorcerer's eyes were suddenly bloodshot and his face looked grey and deathly, as if mortally ill. He continued muttering in an unknown language, spittle flying from his mouth.

"He's gone mad," Mara whispered to Talis, and gripped his arm. "What do we do?"

Talis grimaced, watching the old man getting angrier and more disoriented and confused after each word he spat from his mouth. Nikulo stumbled over, rubbing his head vigorously, casting wary glances at Palarian.

"What's wrong with him? Did the turtle drive him insane?" Nikulo stretched his face wide and blinked several times like he was trying to clear something from his eyes.

"Give him some time," Talis said, and drew characters in the sand with a stick. "See…he's slowly coming out of it, maybe an idea came to him. Whatever happens, we have to make sure he gives us the rune for our world… Let him go home if he wants, he's waited so long."

Palarian stepped somberly towards them, his hands clasped behind his back. When he reached them, he looked up, his eyes black pools of terror.

"I know we must do this thing…but I warn you, there could be dire consequences, to your world and mine. Are you certain you're willing to take the risk?"

"What do you mean…consequences?" Talis wrinkled up his forehead, wondering why the sorcerer was being so cryptic.

"I'm forbidden to tell the story, my father made me swear a sacred vow before the gods. But I can tell you that if we continue on our path and cast the twin portals, there is a chance we'll bring cataclysmic forces to bear on both our worlds. Would you risk it?"

Did they have any other choice? If they didn't cast the portal they'd be stuck here on this world, and Naru would continue to be ruled by Viceroy Lei and the Jiserians. He glanced at Mara for guidance, but she just shrugged her shoulders and looked at him like it was his decision. And Talis knew that the only way of ensuring he got both runes to both worlds was to cast twin portals.

"We take the risk." Talis exhaled, hoping he had made the right choice. "You open a portal to your world and I'll open a portal to ours...we'll do it at the same time. Agreed?"

Palarian chewed on his fingernail, thinking, and finally nodded hesitantly. "Agreed."

Talis pulled off his backpack, and withdrew the blank rune tablets and inscribing tools. He started to hand the runes and tools to Palarian, but the sorcerer raised a finger to stop him.

"You must inscribe your own rune...to your world, and I must create mine with my own tools." The old man snapped his fingers and a blank rune appeared in his left hand and a silver and black inscribing tool in his right. He etched a complicated swirling character onto the rune, sighed as he inspected his work, and displayed it to them. Talis memorized the rune characters, confident he could cast them again in the future...if he ever needed to.

"Vellia...my ancient home...so hard to believe I'll be returning at long last. Now it is your turn, I'll draw the characters for your planet, known to us as Yorek, the world tempted by darkness. Then once completed, we'll simultaneously siphon power from the twin crystals and cast the binding over the runes."

"What if we fail?"

Palarian chuckled brightly. "Then the next moment we'll be standing face to face with the guardians of the Underworld...a quick and painless death. Not even the gift of immortality from the Zacrane Dagger could stop such a death...."

Talis twisted up his face at the idea, but gazed at the sand where the old sorcerer was drawing runes both harsh and simple at the same time.

"Yorek...farewell, world of my banishment, world of my regrets. Though the Isles of Tarasen, cold as they made be, ever warmed my heart. Fondness lingers among those fragrant pines...."

Talis memorized the runes, ever mindful of trickery on the part of the old sorcerer, and inscribed the characters onto the blank tablet. He stared at Palarian until the sorcerer nodded and held the rune ceremoniously towards the north.

"Twin forces, light and darkness, life and death, guide our minds as we bind these twin runes to open portals to twin worlds separated by time and space. We stand here on Chandrix, the stepping stone to many worlds, and give praises to all gods, asking blessings in exchange for our eternal devotion."

Palarian bowed to Talis and closed his eyes. "If the wind stirs from the north, this means the gods are willing, and we each picture our world and cast the binding."

Talis held the tablet tightly and gazed at the empty blackness behind his closed eyes, waiting for a sign from the gods. He felt a fever flush along his back, drops of sweat running down his spine. What if this was a mistake? Was returning home all that important, especially if doing so could risk everything he loved?

But the gods answered with a gust of wind blasting from the north, and the wind felt more like laughter from the gods, a divine trick, laughing at the stupidity of mortals. Talis shrugged off his thoughts and focused on casting the binding spell, picturing the sun-baked streets of Naru, his mother's smile, the hearth-fire at his house, out at the hunt in the swamplands holding Mara's hand.

He was going home.

When he opened his eyes it was as if from a dream, a light-filled one, and the island scene around him had dimmed, a pervasive grey mist suddenly hissing through the air. Charna padded up to him, her tail twitching, golden eyes fearful.

"Now we place the runes and cast the final bindings..." Palarian set the runes on the sand in front of him and mumbled words of prayer.

Talis matched his movements and cast the closing binding spell, his hands trembling like an old man. As the World Portal exploded open in front of him, he glanced desperately at Mara and seized her hand, pulling her close. Nikulo huddled close as well, eyes afraid of the second World Portal churning and scintillating only steps away to their right.

Palarian's eyes were warm and tearful as he stared inside. "We've done it...at long last...Vellia awaits my return...."

A deep rumbling and thundering suddenly sounded in the sky directly above them. The mist had coalesced into thick black and silver clouds crackling with lightning. A huge *pop* sounded above and a third shadow portal formed in the sky, ejecting five flying figures, then it evaporated into nothing.

Aurellia and Rikar descended from the sky, flanked by the three Elder sorcerers Talis had seen at the old Temple of the Sun. Their proud and mocking faces reflected the shivering light of the twin World Portals.

"What have we here?" Aurellia said, studying the portals. "Twin portals? Could it be? And a turtle with twin crystal eyes? Ah...the ancient story is true... And let me guess, one portal leads to Yorek and the other to Vellia."

"A new cycle has begun!" Aurellia shouted, and released twin arcs of electricity from each palm, one aiming at the left portal and the other aiming at the right. He drew his palms together and joined the lightning into one massive arc, clapped his hands together, and the arc remained fixed between the two portals, causing a lightning bridge to form.

Palarian wailed in agony, waving his hands at Aurellia to stop, but the three Elder sorcerers sent shadow cords around his waist and neck and wrists and ankles, and tied the cords onto the iron rod that Palarian had summoned to bind the turtle. Tears streamed from his old, wrinkled eyes as he stared hopelessly into the World Portal that had promised to take him home.

"You pitiful old fool," Aurellia said. "Did you really believe you could kill me so easily? I am ashes and light, a child of death, a mother giving birth to demons. Your thousand years of studying the dark arts was only fodder to fool you into believing you could best me... A perfect ruse."

Aurellia laughed with his eyes but kept his mouth wrinkled and fixed. "You've found the legendary turtle, created by the gods at the founding of this world... I see your magic was sufficient to tame her. And now you share an interconnected fate. She upholds the twin portals through the force of her life, and you, through your magic and power, are fated to keep her alive. If she dies the portals collapse, and your hope of ever returning home dies with it. Keep her alive, faithful servant, and perhaps one day I'll relieve you of your duties and allow you to return home."

Rikar strode over to Talis, his black robe flapping under the north wind, his dark hair long now, eyes black and glowering. He surveyed Talis and Mara and Nikulo slowly, his expression content and pleased. With the flick of his wrist he opened his hand and a stream of golden moths poured into the dark sky, swirling around like fireflies, their wings radiant.

"The wisdom of nightmares brought you here to this world...I feel flattered that you still care for me enough to take the bait. Couldn't stand the idea of me being tortured?"

Talis shook his head. "I pitied you...but what brought me here was Mara. After spending time locked in the Netherworld caves, I pity you even more...."

Rikar scoffed lazily and wagged his finger. "Pity yourself more." He snapped his right finger and a web of shadows screamed out and yanked Mara away from Talis. With Rikar's other hand, hundreds of shadow threads wrapped around Mara's waist and flung her screaming into the World Portal leading to Vellia.

"Mara, no!" Talis shouted. Not into Vellia, it was the wrong portal. But she was gone, and there was nothing he could do except clench his teeth and raise a hand to strike Rikar down, vowing to kill him for what he had done to her.

"Now...now, my loyal apprentices," Aurellia said, chuckling to himself. "Such eagerness and passion! Save it for the mission ahead in Vellia...you will need it. And remember your vow to me, young Talis, you are bound to me...."

The dark lord turned to his Elders. "Faithful Raelles...enter the portal to Yorev and bring word to my loyal sorcerers and necromancers, come join the fight!

"Relech! Rolovian! Through the portal, secure our entry, claim Vellia once again as our own." Aurellia smiled as the wight-like Elders flew into the portal. "Now we leave diligent Palarian to mind the portals as we go to conquer Vellia."

Aurellia motioned Rikar and Nikulo towards the Vellia portal, and turned back to stare at Talis. Charna hissed at Aurellia as he came close, choosing protection inside Talis's arms.

"Your lynx...a gift from the Goddess...interesting... Unfortunately, you're still unprepared for the dangers inside the world ahead...stay close to me, stay close to the Elders, else you and your friends suffer. Go now! On to Vellia, on to victory...."

Talis stumbled towards the Vellia portal, his throat dry, heart heavy; he felt like a ghost walking. He never should've even thought of opening twin portals. At least with the portals open, the Jiserian sorcerers would leave Naru and join the fight in Vellia. Perhaps his family and city would be safe, for the time being. But his world might be in even greater peril in the future....

I swore fealty to a monster, Talis thought. How could he have done it? Death would have been better... Holding Charna tight, he took one more step, and could feel the sickening pull of the Vellia portal as it yanked him aeons away through space.

His first breath in Vellia: the sound of crashing waves, the smell of coconuts roasting, tanned villagers fleeing the ensnaring shadow spells of Rikar and Rolovian and Relech, and Mara cowering behind a wooden boat, shivering despite the heat.

He ran to her, wrapping his arms around her trembling form, and whispered reassuring words in her ear. She nodded and sobbed softly, tears spilling from her eyes. *We'll return home, we'll return home, I promise, someday we will.*

Above the vibrant palm and coconut branches, filtering between lazy clouds meandering across the blue vastness, Talis gaped at three gigantic shapes scarring the sky.

Dragons.

Made in the USA
Lexington, KY
16 June 2013